The Green Hills

The Green Hills

LAURAN PAINE

Sagebrush
Large Print Westerns

Library of Congress Cataloging-in-Publication Data

Paine, Lauran.
   The green hills / Lauran Paine.
      p.   cm.
   Originally published : The green hills / by Nevada Carter.
London : Western Book, C1973.
   ISBN 1-57490-440-X (alk. paper)
   1. Large type books. I. Title

   PS3566.A34 G74 2002
   813'.54—dc21   2002012118

Sagebrush Large Print Westerns are published in the United
States and Canada by Thomas T. Beeler, Publisher, PO Box 659,
Hampton Falls, New Hampshire 03844-0659. ISBN 1-57490-440-X

Published in the United Kingdom, Eire, and the Republic of
South Africa by Isis Publishing Ltd, 7 Centremead, Osney
Mead, Oxford OX2 0ES England. ISBN 0-7531-6695-X

Published in Australia and New Zealand by Bolinda Publishing
Pty Ltd, 17 Mohr Street, Tullamarine, Victoria, Australia, 3043
ISBN 1-74030-666-X

Manufactured by Sheridan Books in Chelsea, Michigan.

The Green Hills

CHAPTER ONE

THAT MAN WHO WENT, TWO WEEKS PAST, SAID THAT everything passed before a man's eyes, and maybe it did for him, but if that proved anything, it was simply what most men already knew about life: it was different from man to man.

The simple things were easiest remembered, like new dawn pouring gold across the cordillera in a hush so deep it reached far down inside a man. Like Old Babe, the sea-brown stringhalt mare who really wasn't much as horses went, but anyone's first live mount was Pegasus's equal.

Like riding into town with honest-to-God earned silver in a pants pocket. Like the look on Paw's face when a young buck rode out his first bucking horse, and the look on Maw's face the day a feller rode home with a squeaky-new shellbelt, holster and Colt, worn loose around a feller's middle.

The grey of Tassie Meredith's eyes and how they darkened and her face colored when she laughed. The soft-gentle touch of her hand, and the fading moonlight, and promises, that seemed to elude a feller, or at least seemed to fade before the stronger call of the things every man had to do sometime in his life; ride off in all the clean, warm sweep of springtime.

What a feller remembered about all those things, and other things too, was that in the background was the town, and beyond it the range, the high country, the lower foothills, the natural beauty of Carter Valley—the green hills of home.

1

All the rest of it lurked elsewhere in a man's mind, willing to rise up if bidden, but neither needed nor heeded. Not even the men a feller knew and warmed to, laughed with and rode with, and were now shadows in a wide grey space that lacked the substance and color of that other place.

The green hills of home. Jason's wistful look when his elder brother saddled up to look beyond the cordillera. How big Jase had grown during a feller's absence, how kind of brooding solemn he had become. How strange they had seemed to one another at the re-meeting in the cemetery when they laid Maw to rest.

How Tassie Meredith had also changed, had filled out, turned round and lost her freckles, and no longer wore her hair in those rusty-auburn braids. But when she laughed it was the same; her eyes darkened and she blushed.

She had grown from the prettiest gangling, freckle-faced tomboy in Carter Valley to the kind of a woman a man could see across a wide room, and feel the pull.

There wasn't a whole lot more. Junction hadn't changed. As a trail-town in Paw's time it had been a hell-roaring place with more acreage in boothill than it had in the entire business district. Paw had said a lot of change had taken place, but then, Paw had come up over forty-five years earlier with a Texas drive, had met Maw and had never again set foot beyond town. Anything changed in forty-five years, but damned few towns changed in something like ten years. Eight, to be exact.

Men changed, people changed, a lot of lesser things changed, but cow-towns didn't change very fast, especially where the population was static and nothing as spectacular as perhaps a gold rush or a land grab or a railroad coming, ever happened.

Junction looked the same a decade later. A few old-timers were gone, which was bound to happen. Old Cappy Dalton, who had worn out a dozen or more good horses with the Secesh raiders during the Civil War, was gone; he would sit by the hour fascinating boys who should have been hurrying on home to do their chores after school, telling awesome tales of Confederate triumphs—always *cavalry* triumphs—and one day when Charley Leavitt, who was a little older, asked how it could be with so many victories, the Secesh had lost the war, old Cappy had looked at them with a wise-sad smile and had said, "Well now, boys, that's somethin' you'll want to remember when your time comes: ain't the fellers who fight wars win or lose 'em, it's the fellers who *talk* aboutfightin' wars that do that."

Cappy promised to leave his big sabre and his old horse-pistol to a feller when he died, but at Maw's funeral Jase said Earl Milner had them now, hanging over the backbar in his saloon. Cappy had changed his mind.

Well, there's always a point where a feller had to stop going back in memory, and that was as good a place as any.

Tassie's paw still owned the general mercantile and the Forsyths still had the forge and buggy works. There *was* one thing added in Junction, a telegraph office. Its inauguration was inadvertently celebrated by a shocking bit of news which had brought home to everyone in Carter Valley how wonderful this new discovery was. The same day that it happened, June 26th, 1876, the defeat and annihilation of George Custer and over two hundred men of his 7th Cavalry was flashed over the telegraph wire, and Junction was stunned.

The telegraph made a difference no one really

3

foresaw; maybe they should have, but old habits died hard and before new ones came thousands of empty miles of open rangeland had been surrounded by a facility that could send news of a killing, of a robbery, or a cattle raid, in all directions faster than the swiftest horse could carry its raiding rider out of reach.

Maybe it was as Preacher Clymer had said at Maw's funeral: those who came and made their mark, then moved on to a better place, left a quieter world where the works of man could flourish in peace and, hopefully, in prosperity.

They hadn't said much to a feller at Maw's funeral. Paw was blind then and hard of hearing. He blew the top off his head the following summer lying flat out in his old wagon, holding a scattergun under his jaw.

It was better to think of times before Maw's burial. Like the time he and Rastus, their coal-black mongrel, had treed a panther cub, and it was so scairt that even Rastus got to feeling sorry for it, and after a feller got it down out of the tree—and it tore his shirt and drew blood with its claws—Rastus licked it. Then they turned it loose and went home, and Maw gave a feller a shellacking with Paw's razor strop for not taking his shirt off *first*, before climbing the consarned tree.

And Tassie had asked why he hadn't wanted to sit on the stump out back of her house in town that same afternoon when he took Jase, who was very small then, to town for a pennyworth of licorice root.

Maw never whipped a feller that she didn't afterwards get so miserable she'd give him a penny. It almost made the larruping worthwhile, almost; Maw had a powerful arm on her.

And the time he and Paw caught some wild horses and peddled them in Junction for two dollars each, then

4

split the money, and he had eight silver cartwheels, more money than he'd known existed in the whole wide world up to that time.

He and Tassie had got sicker'n dogs eating taffy, licorice root, jellybeans, and drinking sarsaparilla. Tassie's father had got mad about that, so, for a month, being a prudent feller, he hadn't gone near their store or their house.

It passed over, like most other things. There were always the green foothills out back of the ranch. A feller could ride his mare out there bareback and lie in the buffler grass and watch how the cloud shapes continually changed. No matter what happened to bring on a misery or a sadness, there were always those green hills of home.

There wasn't much more to recollect. There should have been because twenty-eight years seemed like a long life. Not in comparison to old Cappy Dalton's eighty years, of course, but a feller could cram a heap of living in twenty-eight years, if he worked at it.

But the last eight years of it wasn't worth recalling. About the best a feller could think about those years was that they had been *lived.*

Then the thick, massive shadow of Olin Matthews appeared and his familiar voice, always a little short, a little rasping, said, "Time, Frank. Here, I brought you a pencil and a piece of paper, in case you want to write anything down."

Olin was an ageing, hard-soft man. It was easy to imagine him twenty years back cleaning out a saloon brawl or maybe going bear hunting with a fly swatter. But age had reached down into him, too. He still sounded hard and fearless, but he seemed to have to force it a little now. He handed in the pencil and paper,

5

then opened the door and completely filled the gap, lined and weathered and grey and scarred.

"Take five minutes and write something," Matthews urged. "It can wait that long." Matthews kept lifting his eyes to the little window, then bringing them back. He finally said, "Gawddammit, Frank, I feel about half sick. You feelin' all right?"

Frank rose and put the pencil and paper aside. "I'll make it, Olin. No call for you to feel bad. I don't think it makes a heap of difference whether a man's first or last, does it?"

Matthews considered this, then shrugged mighty shoulders. "Maybe not. You want a drink? I got a pony of apple brandy out front. Maybe you'd better take one, Frank. The lousy buzzards are out there thicker'n hair on a dog's back, waiting."

Frank laughed. "I'm not going to embarrass you, Olin."

"I wasn't thinkin' of *me,* damn it all, boy."

"Well, then, I won't embarrass myself, if that's what you got in mind." Frank picked up his hat and dumped it upon the back of his head, and smiled. "Let's go, Olin."

The green hills of home. The way Tassie blushed when she smiled, Jason following everywhere, worshipping his older brother. Maw's look the day he rode into the yard with his first gun and shellbelt. Paw's proud stance the first time he rode the snap out of a bronc. Cappy's bright, twinkling blue eyes. The old seal-brown stringhalt mare.

Oh Jesus I'm sorry. I'm sorry.

In the springtime Arizona's northward mountains were almost as good to see in morning sunlight as the cordillera of Colorado, but the foothills were dry looking even this early, and the ground roundabout was

6

already turning hard to the shovel and the pick.

Up home the foothills were softer, more rounded, more green and alive with life's constant promise. A feller could lie out there alone in the stands of grass and watch the cloud shapes turn into something different minute by minute.

Despite all the things that happened, a feller could never forget the green hills of home.

CHAPTER TWO

ARCHER GRANT HAD ARRIVED IN JUNCTION, Colorado, as the first telegrapher, and although he was more wizened now than ever, more waspish, and still chewed tobacco with only half the teeth he'd once had, the Great Western Telegraph Company had never seen fit to replace him, and maybe that was a good decision, because Archer, despite some complaints due to age, was still one of the best telegraphers in the territory.

He was irascible, and he was a little self-important, but maybe he was entitled to be that way, too. No one could operate a key like he could, and every momentous event that happened was brought forth under his hand. In a way, Archer Grant was Junction's oracle, and it was almost a certainty that he viewed himself in that light, as now, when he turned to the rawboned, square-jawed man smoking a brown-paper cigarette at the counter, and said, "Marshal, he'll be arriving on the midday stage up from rails-end."

The rawboned man nodded and continued to smoke, and leaned there indolently gazing up towards the faraway rolling foothills. "Then it's all finished," he eventually said, and pulled upright off the counter.

7

"Arch, I feel a thousand years old."

Grant wrinkled his hooked nose. "Good riddance, if you ask me."

The rawboned man looked downward. "I'd keep them thoughts to myself if I was you, Arch."

Grant did not flinch. "Why? All right, I know you and him rode together and all that, but he was nothing but a cold-blooded outlaw and we all know it. And now they're sending him back here to be planted beside his maw and paw. And what about his younger brother? Jason's a right fine man. Why didn't Frank think a little about *that*; about what he was doing to—"

The rawboned man wearing the town marshal's star-and-circlet turned abruptly and walked out into the roadway sunshine. He remembered something Frank Hurd had said one time, when they were range riding for the Sheffield outfit over near Laramie, on the windy plains.

"I got to have more out of life than this, Beau. It's not the work, it's knowing I'm going to end up like those old gaffers round town all crippled up with the miseries and sweepin' out Earl Milner's saloon for eating money. I'm not goin' to ride back with you. I'm goin' on, and by gawd when I *do* come back—well—folks'll look up and nod; it won't be just another saddle tramp ridin' in, next time I get home."

And it hadn't been. Marshal Beaufort—Jedediah Beaufort—remembered very clearly how it had been when Frank had come back. For his mother's burial out back of town. Folks looked up all right; Junction hadn't had a real gunfighter in it since shortly after the lousy Indian wars had ended something like forty years back. Folks looked up all right—but they didn't nod.

Beau went down to the general store and got Howard

8

Meredith, Tassie's father, to one side, to pass along the news. Howard, who was an older man, thick through the middle and balding, said to be the wealthiest man in Junction, had carried the cross of his daughter's feeling for the gunfighter Frank Hurd without ever trying to conceal it any more than he did now. He looked at Beau with a pained scowl and said, "I wish to hell this would *end*. Why didn't they just bury him down in Arizona and have done with it?"

"Because Jase wanted him brought home," replied the town marshal. "And I don't blame him."

"Well," mumbled Howard Meredith, "All right. But after today I don't ever want to hear his name again."

Beau's face was impassive. "You'll be out at the cemetery, won't you, Howard?"

Meredith fidgeted. "Yes, damn it, I'll be out at the burying, Beau. Now excuse me, I got a shipment out back to be off-loaded."

Beau left the old store building and nearly collided with Jim Forsyth, who did the blacksmithing now that his father was getting along. The elder Forsyth worked almost exclusively in the next door wagon works. Beau and Jim and Frank Hurd had grown up together.

"Frank'll be comin' in on the stage directly," Beau said. "You'll be out there, won't you, Jim?"

Forsyth, who was a solid six-footer with an expression of confidence and assurance, nodded. "Yeah . . . What a hell of a way to see Frank again."

"You won't see him, Jim. They always bolt the boxes closed, on hanged men."

"I didn't mean *look* at him, Beau. You remember that time we took Clymer's topbuggy and got it up astraddle the ridgepole of his house on Halloween?"

Beau's eyes flickered briefly. "I never got such a

9

threshing from my paw as I did the next morning. Yeah, I remember. By the way, Jim, I haven't got time to go out and tell Jason at the ranch. You got a man down at the shop you could send out?"

From the doorway of the general store behind Marshal Beaufort a quiet voice said, "I'll go." Both men turned.

Tassie, at twenty-two, almost twenty-three, was a genuine spinster—which was something else that deeply troubled her father, who was not getting any younger, and had no sons to take over the mercantile business. She was also every bit as lovely as Frank Hurd had remembered her being.

It had long been a topic of discreet talk round town that Tassie Meredith was wasting her life, waiting for Frank Hurd. Well, now the waiting was almost over.

"I was going to drive out that way this afternoon, anyway. I'll just harness up a little earlier," she told the two sturdy men. She smiled at them because they looked so stonily miserable. "I can make it through one more day. You two ought to be able to, also. Beau—I don't have any tears left."

Jim Forsyth shifted his feet. "I'll go harness the mare for you, Tassie." He turned and escaped, but Beau was left there. He knew—*everyone* knew—she'd had at least a dozen proposals since turning seventeen, and before that she'd had cowboys standing one on top of another in her father's store buying things they didn't need, to maybe get a chance to make her smile. She had never stopped loving Frank Hurd, the gunfighter who became an outlaw. Never. She *still* loved him.

Beau let his breath out softly. Frank had been his partner, his friend, his confidante; he had always liked Frank Hurd. He still liked the Frank Hurd he had known. But ten thousand Frank Hurds didn't deserve *this*. She was more woman than a man would find in five years of steady looking.

She smiled upwards at Beau. "It's like closing a book, isn't it? How many are left around who really knew him, Beau?"

There was a harsh answer to that; Beau had been a lawman for the same number of years Frank had been a gunman, so he knew the subsequent Frank Hurd even though he never saw him again, up until his mother's funeral. But a man couldn't say anything like that, and especially to someone like Tassie, so Beau simply bobbed his head and sought for a fresh topic.

"You might have to drive out west of the ranch to find Jase. This time of year they always drove the cattle into the foothills."

Tassie understood. "I know. I used to help them, when Frank was home."

Beau took down a big breath. "Tassie. Get it out of your system. Frank's dead."

Her gaze darkened a little. "You don't have to tell me that, Beau. I knew it would happen long before it did happen. That's what I meant a minute ago when I said I don't have any tears left. I don't think I can cry out there this afternoon. This will be sort of like closing the barn after the horses are gone. But Beau—tell me how a person gets something out of their system that's been there since I first looked across the slate when we were little kids, and saw him sitting there, over by the window at the schoolhouse?"

Beau said, "I wish it could have been me."

She accepted this. "I wish it could have been, too, Beau. You or Jim, or Pete Clymer, or that nephew of Earl Milner's who came out and lived a year with his

11

uncle." She turned at the sound of her father's voice from within the store, then smiled again and was gone.

Beau walked towards the buggy works, and from there he went to the saddle and harness shop, then over to the gunsmith's store, and gradually he spread the word throughout town. Mostly, the people said they would be out there for Frank Hurd's burying, but no one had said it as though they were doing it for Frank. The older people were doing it for the memory of Frank's parents, and a few were doing it for Jase. Of course there were some, mostly younger people or late comers, who were going to attend the burying out of curiosity. Frank hadn't got quite as notorious as that feller Bonney down in New Mexico, or the James brothers, but he was well on the way to becoming that notorious when they cornered him in Tucson and beat him unconscious, then jailed him and put in a claim for the reward before trying, and hanging him.

Beau was out front of Milner's saloon standing there with Earl, idly talking, when Tassie Meredith went wheeling northward up the road out of town heading for the Hurd place. She did not look over, but Beau understood perfectly well that she had seen them. Earl, who was older and therefore presumably wiser, said, "It'll be like peeling a whole chapter out of her life, this afternoon. You realize that, Beau?"

There was no reason to answer any question like that; it didn't need answering, it was too obvious, so Beau kept watching as the yellow undercarriage of her topbuggy flashed in golden sunlight, then, after she was half a mile up the road, he shook his head a little at Milner.

"Sometimes it's awful hard to figure things out, Earl."

12

Milner looked at the spidery hands of his pocket watch. "What things?"

"Nothin'," answered Beau, and would have walked on but the saloon keeper detained him with a question.

"You'd better send someone out there early to get the hole dug, hadn't you? If the stage delivers that damned box and we got to leave it sittin' in the street in the back of someone's wagon all afternoon, it's not going to look right, is it?"

Beau agreed and departed, heading for the livery barn. Two hostlers down there dug graves for a dollar each. They still had plenty of time, though. In the 'old days' when Beau and Frank had been youngsters hovering around wherever old Cappy Dalton sat in the sunshine, there hadn't been a telegraph office in Junction; in those days the stage would simply have arrived, unloaded the pine box, and *then* folks would have started making arrangements to dig the hole.

That same damned telegraph that had enabled the law down at Tucson to identify Frank Hurd as a wanted man, and which was therefore at least partially responsible for his being in that damned pine box, was now doing him a small favor by enabling Junction to be prepared for tucking him away without an awkward and embarrassing delay.

If there was some kind of compensation there, Beau couldn't quite find it. A little delay to a man stone dead in a rough slab coffin couldn't be much of an embarrassment. At least not to the man in the box. But if that lousy telegrapher hadn't been so zealous at his key, well, Frank would still be alive.

But that was no good either. Frank had gone down his personal road too far to ever turn back. Maybe, just maybe, this was best after all. Best for Tassie, for Jason,

13

for Beau and for Jim Forsyth—maybe even best for Frank; at least that thing he'd feared so much, that matter of growing old and crippled and destitute, hadn't happened.

But gawd a'mighty, twenty-eight was so *young* to be leaving!

They were down there waiting for Beau because the news of Frank's coming had spread very fast, once it had come over the wire. Normally, the hostlers, rough, crude men, made some kind of little joke about the way they earned their dollar. Today, having been forewarned by their employer, they simply agreed to go right out and commence digging. That was all there was to it. For two dollars Frank Hurd got his homecoming.

CHAPTER THREE

THERE WERE TREES AT THE CEMETERY OUT BACK OF town, and there were two separate areas out there, one for family plots and respected citizens, the other area, which was the 'boothill' division, for men, mostly drovers and cowboys, with an occasional gambler, horse thief or rustler, who died violently.

In the permanent section the stones were granite, and some of the graves had little mortar kerbings around them, while in the boothill section the markers—and many were gone now—had been made of wood with a number of the names denoting only that "Butch" or "Rawhide" or "Horse thief Called Smith" lay below.

It was perhaps symbolic of the times that no one had been buried in the boothill section in quite a few years, but quite a number of upstanding folks had been interred in the other section.

14

In wintertime the cemetery was a dreary place, what with the graves covered with wildly tumbling brown leaves, the grass gone brown, and the trees standing in the wind like skeletons chained in place while the elements scourged them left and right. But in spring and summer there was warmth and color and shade from the high spreading trees. There was birdsong and fragrance until the entire atmosphere was not of finality, but was rather of recurring promise.

It was that kind of a day when they put down Frank Hurd. The people had walked out from town—the distance was only about a half mile, maybe a little less—to stand in solemn array while Claude Clymer preached a quiet service—not about Frank especially, but about forgiveness and salvation and streets of gold and eternal summertime.

Then they lowered the box and Jase stepped forward, big and strained and self-conscious, dressed in his suit, which was dark, and trickled downward a handful of earth while Preacher Clymer murmured something about from dust to dust.

Someone back in the silent throng kept fighting back sneezes, which was the only sound except for Preacher Clymer's voice; there were a lot of nettles along the cemetery fence, along with cottonwood pollen and ragweed, so if a person was bothered by hayfever, the cemetery was a mighty poor place to be.

The walk back was almost as solemn as the walk out, and as the burial ceremony had been. Archer Grant, mincing along beside big Howard Meredith, leaned and softly said, "Pity they buried him atween his maw and paw, who was respectable folk, don't you think?"

Meredith did not reply. He stalked along stonily impassive with little beads of perspiration upon his

15

balding head. Up ahead his daughter was pacing along with big Jason Hurd, and Meredith, who was not a man entirely without feeling, was pained for her. He also felt discomfort for Jason, who had an account at the store and was a man of his word if one ever lived. If Howard Meredith wondered at all, it was not about Frank, except indirectly, it was about how two people like the elder Hurds could have brought forth two such different sons.

But most of all, Howard Meredith was relieved that it was all over now; no matter how Tassie had loved Frank, it was finished, and what had worried Meredith the most—the thought that Frank might send for his daughter, and that she might have gone to him—was over, too.

Now, given enough time, she would have to recover, which meant she might find another young buck. Meredith certainly hoped she would, and soon.

Folks spread out once they reached town, most of them, like the Forsyths and Earl Milner, heading for home so they could get out of their suits and stays and get back into comfortable, everyday attire.

Beau, who had brushed his hat clean, went to the jailhouse office and shed his coat and tie, and considered the immaculate hat, which looked almost as good as when he had originally bought it four years back, over at Meredith's store. It was the sixth time in four years he'd brushed it like that, each time it had been for a funeral.

He made a pot of coffee on the woodstove and took a cup to the window and gazed out into the sunshine and shade. Jase and Tassie were talking, out front of her father's store. Jase looked almost handsome in his dark suit, with his hard, big frame standing loose and with his tanned face lowered while he listened.

16

Tassie always looked handsome, but in that dark dress with the wide-brimmed hat, holding her black gloves and with slanting sun rays making her red-rusty hair glint like new money, she was a picture.

Beau finished the coffee and turned back to the litter of his desk top. Being a town marshal, normally, was routine, but every now and then—usually this time of year, in the spring—wanted posters began trickling in as the outlaw business picked up with the advent of decent weather.

Otherwise, though, Junction was a quiet, law-abiding place. Of course, springtime also brought in the range riders, either passing through northward on their way to promised jobs, or fanning out over Carter Basin seeking work with local cow outfits, and these men were usually, to a more or less degree, troublesome.

But it was a little early for that. Cowboys usually had to put in a month or six weeks of hard work before accumulating enough pay for a wild night in town up at Milner's saloon. When a man had been keeping the peace around a town as long as Beau had in Junction, he could almost predict the night trouble would come, and the kind of trouble it would be; a fight between a couple of drunks or, maybe, at the worst, a brawl between riders of opposing outfits.

Gunfights were rare. Range men were not as wild and trigger happy as they had once been. There had been no really serious trouble, in fact, since Beau had hired on, and today was no time to be thinking about it anyway; after Frank's funeral, the town was as subdued as he had ever seen it. It was not an easy thing, judging a man they had all known, and whom many of them had liked, and who had died at the end of a rope as an outlaw. *That* part wasn't hard to judge—the outlaw and hanging

17

part—but the death part *was* hard to came to grips with. Every funeral opened a door on to a vista of complete darkness; it made people ponder; they would never be outlaws and they would not die at the end of a rope, but they *would* die, there was no escaping *that*, so now they weren't in a very cheerful mood. Frank knew something they didn't know; that was what contributed most to the solemnity.

Maybe Tassie had it right when she spoke to Jason out front of the store. "There is no place for regrets, now. I don't believe Frank has any, Jason. Somewhere, he's going to be able to start over and I'm happy for him for that."

Jase was not a religious man, and he was even less of a philosopher. Like Howard Meredith, Jase had been carrying a heavy load for a long time, since it had first been verified that the rumors were correct, that Frank had become a professional gunfighter, and, later, also a professional outlaw.

A lot of that load had been left out there at the cemetery, but not all of it. Jase knew nothing of the term 'guilt by association' but he had that kind of a feeling, so he said, "You're probably right, Tassie, but it's over only for Frank."

She understood. "In time it'll end for you, too. People will forget. Anyway, they never thought you were that much like him—like what he became, Jason."

Jase raised his eyes. "A few years back, did you hear about what happened to Edwin Booth, the actor—brother to John Wilkes who shot President Lincoln?"

Tassie had heard; it had been common knowledge at the time. Some miners somewhere out in California, or was it Nevada, beat Edwin Booth very severely, because he was the brother of the assassin who had killed

18

Abraham Lincoln. Archer Grant and a few others had approved, but most folks hadn't.

"But Frank wasn't that well known," she replied. "And he didn't kill anyone as prominent as President Lincoln."

Jase said, "That's not the point, Tassie. The point is that all Edwin Booth had to do was say the wrong thing by accident, do something on the spur of the moment that anyone else could have done and no one would have looked twice. You see? All I have to do is make some kind of a mistake . . . Maybe even vote for the wrong man in an election. You know what folks'll say: What can you expect from the brother of Frank Hurd!"

Tassie did not argue. She was not argumentative by nature, but more importantly, she knew Jason would have to live with the shame of his brother exactly as she would have to also live with it.

She had done a lot of thinking over the past few years; it had forced her to mature faster than she probably ordinarily would have. Any kind of deep pain and grief does that to people.

"Then you do what you are convinced is best, Jase. You're *you*, and people like and respect you. What Frank was simply has to be part of it, doesn't it? You're not the only one."

Jason's tough, steady gaze lingered on her. He was, by nature, a quiet, even-tempered man with a hidden streak of humor and a feeling for things and people. He knew what she meant.

"I'll tell you something, Tassie: You're about the prettiest woman I've ever seen. There've been times when I could have hated Frank right easy, for lousing up your life. By rights you should have been married by now, and be hauling your kids down off the barn roof,

19

and whaling the tar out of them for picking up words down by the corral where the cowhands work."

She smiled. "It's not a duty, Jase. It's something a woman does when she knows everything is right for it. Maybe we wouldn't have married if Frank had stayed home and worked the ranch with you. I'll never know, will I?" She turned as the thick, impatient form of her father appeared in the yonder doorway. "I'll drive out soon," she said, and walked away.

Jase, who had left his saddle animal at the livery barn, trudged on across the road, and people who saw him, who knew him well enough to speak, which they normally would have done, managed to be looking in a window or passing through a doorway. Not to avoid him exactly, but because this was a day when Jase would prefer not having to stop and talk about the weather or cattle prices, or the prospect of good feed in the foothills, and people understood exactly.

Beau did not have an opportunity to avoid the meeting. He was leaving the jailhouse when Jason came along. They looked squarely at one another. Jase stopped and Beau, groping for words, said, "I got a fresh pot of coffee inside."

Jason shook his head. "No thanks, Beau." Their eyes held. "Well, we got him put down, didn't we?"

Beau heard the bitterness, and nodded. "He's got no more troubles, Jase. Figure it that way." Without any change in the timbre of his voice, Beau then said, "We had some good times, years back, Frank and me. He was good with little kids, Jase. He used to drag you around with him like you were a puppy dog. Used to wipe your nose and get you jelly beans when you'd commence whining."

Jason looked down the road in the direction of the

livery barn as he said, "Let's talk about something else." His eyes were hot and dry and dark with pain. "How's the law business, Beau?"

"Quiet, the way I like for it to be. But I reckon it'll heat up. Have you hired on any riders?"

Jase replied with the tightness leaving his voice. "A couple. Young fellers, seem like good men. Both of them are pretty savvy."

"Going to hire any more?"

"No. The three of us can do whatever's got to be done. We finished taking the cattle to the foothills yesterday. We'll get the wagon ready and maybe go back up there next week to commence the branding and marking . . . Beau, Frank sure was good with a rope. You remember that?"

"Yeah, I remember how good he was with a rope. And with mean horses and wild cattle." Beau sighed. "I got to get up to the store, Jase. *Adios*."

Jason went the rest of the way to the livery barn got his horse and without another word to anyone, rode northward up through town on the way home. Far off, in the golden late day the green hills looked softer than he had seen them look since the previous springtime.

Odd how a grown man could feel towards some plain old rolling grassy foothills. Frank used to call them the green hills of home, and he loved them. Hurd cattle had been going up there for spring and summer pasture for as many years as Jason could remember. The hills didn't belong to the Hurd ranch; they didn't belong to anyone, really, but by common understanding the other cowmen did not trespass up there; that was Hurd range.

21

CHAPTER FOUR

IT WAS NOT IMPLYING THAT THE SECOND AND THIRD generations could never have got the land and cattle without help, but it was a plain fact that when someone like Jason's father and mother had acquired the land and began building up the herd, when Jase took over after their passing all he had to worry about, really, was completing the herd build up, and holding everything together, and that took less talent, as everyone knew, than putting the outfit together in the first place. Even Jason agreed with that.

He told Tassie one time that the third generation came off best. The first generation acquired plenty of land for next to nothing. The second generation—Jase's time—finished putting the herd together. The third generation only had to learn how to supervise things, and they had the best of it.

The Hurd place was not one of the largest cow outfits in Carter Valley. There were three or four bigger ones. But the Hurd ranch either owned or controlled some of the best land west of Junction, and northward all the way back up beyond the rolling foothills. It made almost as much money for its owner as did any of the bigger outfits, that had to hire about six or eight riders, and had to pay on mortgages.

It was a good, compact ranch. The log barn was large, sound, and durable. The bunkhouse, where Jason's two riders lived, and batched, which meant they did their own cooking, as well as the old main house, the shoeing shed, the smokehouse and the wagon shed, all were made of peeled fir logs. The corrals, too, were strong

22

and well kept.

It was, as Mike Howell and Red McClure, Jason's two riders, had agreed between them, one of those practically trouble free, well organized outfits where three men could do as much as four, and do it quicker.

McClure was a quarter-breed with dark hair and eyes, and a quiet, good-natured disposition. Mike Howell had a prominent Adams apple, a somewhat reddish tinge to his hair and face, and was tall and thin, and as quick as a striking snake.

It was Howell who saw Jason returning from town after the funeral, and nudged the quarter-breed. "It's over with," he said, "now maybe he'll quit brooding and we can get some work done around here."

McClure turned black eyes. "What work? We don't have nothing to do until we go up and start marking, in a week or two."

Howell spat amber, shifted his chaw, and leaned upon the corral's top stringer as he replied, "You figure a place like this renews itself? Well, it don't. Them buildings gets oiled, the springs get dunged out, the range gets rode, and—"

McClure grinned. "Was you ever a foreman, Mike, or do you just naturally act like an owner?"

Howell, still watching the oncoming horseman, said, "I reckon for the balance of today, and maybe tomorrow, we'd best just keep clear of him and find things to do without asking."

McClure, also squinting across the range, thought that sounded about right. "We could get the wagon out, prop it up and service it for the summer."

Howell pushed off the corral and headed across the yard with the 'breed. "You know, every once in a while a dumb redskin will come up with a good idea."

23

McClure laughed. "Just not very often is all. But you got to remember, we're just catchin' on. We only been wearin' cloth pants about a hunnert years."

They got along well. Neither was thin-skinned, and because all range riders graduated from a rough school, were basically simple and uncomplicated men; with only a few 'don'ts' to watch out for, their lives were rarely concerned with things more involved than what Howell and McClure set about doing now—hoisting a battered wagon with a grub box tailgate and a patched canvas stretched over ash bows—upon some log sawhorses. By the time Jase rode in they already had the wagon in place and were rummaging in the shoeing shed for something to use to get the hub nuts off with.

Jase dismounted out front of the barn and called over. "There's an iron wrench hanging on a peg behind the forge. And remember, those nuts came off *reverse* to the way the wheels turn. I'll be back in a little while."

He put up his horse then went over to the main house to shed his suit and get back into boots and work pants and his checkered flannel shirt. He left the gun and shellbelt hanging on their wall peg. The most completely useless implement when a man was working around was a gun in a hip holster. Not only useless, but heavy.

He went back out into the yard, stood for just a fleeting second glancing northward towards the distant green foothills, felt a little pain of regret, then he clumped down the steps and hiked over where Mike and Red were loosening a wheel nut with the iron wrench and a big wooden mallet. When he came up the cowboys both studied him. He understood, and to put their minds at rest, he smiled at them, then, without a word, took the wrench, reversed it on the nut, tapped a couple of times and the nut loosened.

Howell reddened. "Oh yeah, I remember now. You said them things come off opposite from the way the wheel turned."

McClure went after the wooden bucket with the black grease and wooden paddle, also kept in the shoeing shed. While he was gone neither Jason nor Mike spoke. They had to strain together to lift off the wheel, and that was no time for talk even if either one of them had wanted to speak, and neither of them did.

The rear wheels, much larger and therefore much heavier, required the combined effort of all three men, but off they came, too. Then McClure slathered on the black grease with his wooden paddle after Jase examined the leathers, found them good enough to be left on, and all four wheels were replaced, the nuts— usually called burrs—tightened, and the wagon was ready for another season. There was a deep black scar in the form of the letters JH burned into the wagon on both sides beneath the high driver's seat. JH stood for Joseph Hurd, Jason's father. The ranch was still using those same big old clumsy irons on the cattle and horses. Now, JH stood for Jason Hurd, the last of the line.

Not all cowboys liked shoeing horses, but they knew how to do it. The only ones who were excused were men with bad backs; it was a chore that could keep a man walking hitched up in back for several days afterwards. Jase asked Howell how his back was, and Mike, who disliked shoeing, knew McClure was listening, so he said his back was as strong as any man's damned back in the whole of Carter Valley, and he would have said that if his back had been broken right then at that moment, because what cowboys lacked in brains, they certainly never lacked in pride of manhood.

25

Jason said, "Suppose we saddle up and go drive in the horses and commence shoeing, then." He looked at Red. "Is your back all right?"

McClure grinned. His skin was fair, almost as fair as Jason's skin, but his jet-black eyes and hair were the giveaway. "My back's stout enough," he answered. "It's my hands that ache afterwards."

Howell snorted. "They're all like that; rather be skulkin' around elk hunting than doin' an honest day's labor."

Jase smiled as Red McClure hauled up very erect, and said, "White man got forked tongue."

The three of them went down to the barn, and back a yard or two Red and Mike exchanged a knowing wink; they wouldn't have to avoid Jase for a day or two after all. All they would want to do was be careful of what they said.

There were four stalled horses to be rigged out and straddled. Before leaving to ride west in search of the saddle stock, they opened the sixteen-foot main corral gate, then rode off. That was the only gate with ready access to the range. Inside, a number of smaller gates gave access to several other, smaller working corrals.

It was actually a might late in the day for this kind of work. The sun was already down in the west and while there would be another couple of hours of light, dusk would be arriving before too long.

Still, Jason wanted to move, to work, to be occupied, and whether Mike and Red understood why this was or not, day's end meant little to them in any case. Range men worked when they could and when they had to, and most of them did not carry watches, and those that did invariably forgot to wind them.

For Jason, everything was as it should have been,

except that, along with his usual little sense of gravity and sadness, he rode now with an additional sensation of loss and finality. He said little and thought a lot, but he was in a familiar place doing a commonplace thing, which was some kind of surcease, some kind of an outlet for the natural frustrations that arose from an inability to understand *why*.

They found the horses on their upland, northeasterly sweep along the base of the distant foothills, in a place they wouldn't have expected to find them; grazing along with the cattle. By then dusk was settling downward from the far-curving, hulking massiveness of the cordillera.

Jason knew the ranch horses as well as he knew people, and pointed to a big brown, long-faced horse who stood somberly watching as the riders approached. "Keep an eye on him. He's a ridgling and he's got more brains than most people. He'll start out like a lamb and the first hill we come round, he'll duck out of sight and head straight back up here."

It happened exactly that way, except that when the ridgling slipped around the little hillock, Red was waiting for him with a grin. The ridgling *was* clever, he didn't try to outrun the man on horseback, as a mare would have done, and he didn't lay back his ears or otherwise show disgust and resentment, he simply turned back and went plodding along in the wake of the other animals. He was not a young horse and he knew the futility of spending his energy in something he could not undo.

They got back to the ranch in the early night. The ridgling plodded right on up through the big gate leading the other horses on into captivity, and immediately after Jase swung down and closed the gate,

27

the ridgling went over to the side of the corral nearest the barn and nickered for hay.

The men laughed at him. He seemed to be saying, 'All right, I led them in for you, now pitch some hay in here.'

Mike and Red took the saddle animals to the barn while Jason went after a fork to do as the ridgling had ordered.

The day ended, Jason went on back to the main house, Red and Mike took their time at the barn before heading for the bunkhouse, and a clear moon rose to brighten the long hush to come, while a rash of high stars formed into visible, age-old patterns and clusters. The huge mountains that curved around to the east and west, and which stood miles thick and lumpy, due north, cut out part of the purple vault of night—and less than a half mile out a leg-weary saddle horse plodded along with its limp rider, groggy from distance and tucked up from lack of feed and care.

Some coyotes yapped on their nightly foray down into the foothills, where they wouldn't find much because all the calving was over this late in the year, while farther back, not as brazen, a wolf sat on his gaunt haunches and sounded the loneliest cry of them all; of all four-legged predators he had been hunted, and feared the most for more centuries than anyone knew. That he still existed was a marvel.

Jase heard him and went out front to the porch to assess the sound for direction. Coyotes would not harm calves, especially if the wicked horned mother cows were around, but a wolf had more courage; he would outrun a calf, outfight the cows, and kill anything up to five or six hundred pounds.

It was a chilly night, like most Colorado nights were,

with the stars down close enough, almost, for a man to be able to reach out and touch them. Every sound was carried and multiplied.

He stood out there waiting for the wolf to sound again, and when he failed to do that, Jase stood still, looking towards the blacked-out foothills, his thoughts aimlessly turning first one way, then another way, and finally they recapitulated the events of this day, which probably was inevitable.

There was no excuse for Frank, really, when a man came right down to the basics of it. He would have inherited the ranch; he was his mother's firstborn and his father's pride, and Jase would have cheerfully worked the place with him. They had always got on well.

A horse nickered out in the darkness northwest of the barn, which brought Jase's thoughts back to the present. He did not believe they had missed one in the drive, but it was possible. Anyway, even if it was someone's stray, come morning it would be standing outside the corrals.

Jase returned to the house, tired all the way through.

CHAPTER FIVE

IT WASN'T EVEN LIGHT YET WHEN MCCLURE CAME scratching at the front door, managing to project a sense of urgency on through to where an awakening Jason Hurd was grudgingly struggling up through layers of warmth and comfort to heed the sound.

The scratching persisted. Jase swore up out of bed, pulled on his britches, stamped into his boots, and picked up his shirt as he went out through the big old parlor with its massive stone fireplace to the door. He shrugged into the shirt one-armed as he flung back the door and peered out.

McClure sounded breathless. "You'd better come down to the barn. There's a feller in one of the mangers down there."

Jase scowled. "A what?"

"A feller. Some feller come in last night, late, Mike figures, and bedded down in a manger in the barn. You'd better come along."

Jase pushed McClure back, stepped out and craned around. There was a faint glimmer of light coming out from the big, doorless front opening down there. He turned back.

"What in the hell . . . ?"

McClure fluttered his hands. "I don't know, Boss. Stranger to me. But he's in pretty bad shape. You'd better come. I got to fetch some hot water from the bunkhouse." McClure retreated down off the porch and went loping off through the darkness in the direction of the bunkhouse.

Jason buttoned his shirt, shoved it inside his waistband, and almost followed McClure. At the last moment he turned back, went to his bedroom, took down the gun and belt and strode more briskly back outside while he buckled the belt in front.

It was the coldest time of night—or morning—and usually it was also the most hushed and still. Tonight was no exception. Jase heard only the grind of his own foot-falls across the yard.

At the barn he found Mike bending over something that had been laid out upon the ground inside one of the horse stalls. The lantern was guttering because its wick needed trimming. Jase went on over and looked down.

McClure hadn't exaggerated, it was a man, and he

was in poor shape. Even in that ghostly brightness it was possible to see how white and sweaty the stranger's face was, how limp and gauntly flat his body lay.

Jase dropped to one knee as Mike twisted towards him, his Adams apple bobbing very noticeably as he spoke. "Never seen him before. I was just comin' awake this morning and heard some horses squealin' down here, like maybe one was inside the corral and the other one was fighting him over the fence. I come out to look around." Howell turned and pointed. "There's the horse. I brought him in and tied him up. He ain't in too good a shape, either. I was goin' to tie him in this stall, then I seen this feller." Mike dropped his arm, lifted the front of the stranger's riding jacket, lifted his torn shirt, and Jason's breath caught short in his throat.

"Been shot," said Mike Howell. "Looks like it was some time back. Maybe three, four days back." Mike eased the shirt and jacket closed. "He's in damned poor shape, Boss."

Red came hurrying with a bucket of hot water off the bunkhouse stove, some rags, and a flat little pony-bottle of whisky. He squinted over Howell's shoulder. "Still alive?"

Mike nodded and took the whisky first. Jason helped by lifting the man's head and shoulders. They spilled more than they got down him, but he swallowed a couple of times. He had to; it was swallow or strangle.

Jason pulled some hay from the manger and bunched it under the man's head and made him comfortable that way, then he watched as Mike bared the man's chest and went to work swabbing away the caked and fresh blood with rags soaked in hot water.

Red stood like a statue for a moment or two, then bent and lifted out the stranger's sixgun, opened the gate

31

and gently turned the cylinder. "Three empties," he announced, and handed the weapon to Jason. "Whoever shot him probably didn't come off too well, neither."

It was a safe guess. Even unconscious and as limp as a sack of grain, the stranger looked rangy, tough, and capable. He was not a very old man, probably no older than Jase was. His face, though, showed a definite hardness, a definite strength of character that seemed, perhaps, to tend towards harshness and possibly even cruelty.

Mike finished cleaning the wound and wrinkled his nose. "In his fix I'd have hunted up the nearest town and got myself to a doctor. I can feel the rib bones grind together. How far you reckon he could have rode like that?"

Jason had no idea, but he knew one thing for a fact. If the horse he'd heard nicker the night before, to the northwest, had been carrying this man, and if it had come down-country from the mountains, then this stranger hadn't been near a town for at least four days, because that was how long it took a rider to cross those mountains.

McClure said, sounding solemn, "He won't make it. The bullet's still in him, ain't it, Mike?"

Howell, who had been examining the wound, lifted the bony points of his shoulders and let them drop. "Don't know, Red. Looks like the slug hit him halfway in front, and sort of ploughed around with the curve of his body. Maybe he was moving, maybe turning or something like that, when he got hit. But I'll tell you one thing, if that bullet hadn't carved him open, if it'd ploughed right on through, straight, the way it was supposed to, he'd never have got on his horse, let alone rode this far. He'd have been killed an the spot."

Jase moved to the stranger's far side and when Mike reared back on his heels, Jason leaned down and with his finger probed along the swollen, ragged-edged slash. "It's not still in him," he said. "Like you figure, Mike, it followed on around. It went out from beneath the hide, low there, on the left side." Jason straightened back. "But he's lost a hell of a lot of blood."

Howell watched Jason. "Can't move him. Sure as hell he'll die."

Jason wasn't concerned much about moving the man. "He'll probably die anyway," he stated, and got stiffly back up to his feet. "Damned wonder he didn't fall off his horse somewhere in the mountains or out on the range. If he had, no one would have found him until the buzzards started circling." Jason motioned. "Empty his pockets while I go look at the horse."

The animal was dull and listless and head-hung as Jase removed the saddle and bridle, flung them aside and took the horse outside where dawn was beginning to show in watery streaks in the east. He put the horse in a corral separate from the other animals and went back to get it a big forkful of hay. The horse started to eat, and as long as Jase walked around looking at him, he did not raise his head. He was half starved, but he was a good animal; young, liver-chestnut in color, well muscled, with a good head and neck, and a nice eye.

He was not marked, which was the first thing Jase looked for. At least not until Jase patted his neck and ran a hand up under the full mane did he see any sign of a brand. Even then he would have missed it, hidden like that up under the mane on the left side of the neck, if his fingertips hadn't felt the slightly raised lesions where the iron had sizzled. He bent, looked, then stepped back and leaned upon the corral, pondering. The mark was a small, neat pair of letters. US. Any time a man in civilian clothes rode a young, sound, valuable horse branded US, it was a very strong possibility that someone, probably the rider himself, had stolen it, because the Army did not ordinarily sell cavalry mounts, and it never sold tractable, sound, young ones.

Jase returned to the barn and went to examine the saddle and bridle. There was a tight little professional blanket roll behind the cantle, but no saddlebags. The saddle itself had no maker's name on it, although it probably had had one; the seating leather was a replacement, obviously, the leather was much lighter than the rest of the saddle. Saddle makers commonly put their names up where the seating leather was carved out behind the gullet on the seating leather.

Jase looked over the bridle. It told him nothing at all except that it had seen a lot of service. He unrolled the blanket roll and a small, nickel-plated under-and-over .41 caliber Derringer tumbled out. Otherwise, there was a complete change of clothes, two blankets, the ground-sheet itself, which was what the blanket roll had been rolled in, and two boxes of cartridges, one for a sixgun, one for a carbine. But the stranger had had no carbine and there was no boot buckled to his saddle.

That was all. No letters, no writing material, no pencils even, and nothing that would have made it possible for the stranger to have identified his blanket roll from a hundred others just like it.

He returned to the place where Red McClure had everything from the unconscious man's pockets in a sweat stained black hat. He handed all this to Jase, who saw the letters burned into the sweatband of the hat. J.B.

Mike said, "Hoist his head again, one of you fellers. We can get another couple of swallows of likker down him anyway."

Jase put the hat aside and leaned to comply. This time, the whisky went down easier, and afterwards, as Jase was lowering the man's head, he groaned hoarsely.

"Comin' round," said Mike, leaning down to lift an eyelid and look closer. He was correct, but not right then. It was a minute or two later that Jase happened to look upwards and saw the sunken set of eyes staring at him. Jase groped for something to say.

"You lost a lot of blood, mister. We got some whisky down you. Otherwise, when we can take the chance, we'll pack you into the bunkhouse."

The stranger lay silent, his chest faintly rising and falling. He turned sluggishly and regarded both McClure and Howell, then he closed his eyes, sighed, and turned loose all over.

McClure said, "Dead. He just left us."

Mike placed his head to the man's chest and while Jason waited, Mike strained for the faint beat. It was still there, but as Howell hauled away he said, "Not yet, Red, but I sure wouldn't want to bet no money on how soon."

The stranger's dry, hot lips parted a fraction. "Odds— aren't—good, cowboy, are they?"

Mike was flustered. He obviously hadn't thought he'd be heard. But he had to answer so he said, "Depends on which way you want to go, I reckon. Folks manage to drag through sometimes when they don't have no right to. What I meant was . . ."

"Got—some more of—that rotgut whisky?" whispered the injured man, and McClure handed over the bottle, but when Mike would have given the man another drink Jase said, "No. He's had enough. We're not going to get him drunk, just back breathing again."

35

Jase leaned down. "Mister, can you swallow food?" He got no answer, not even a flicker to indicate that he had been heard, but he looked around at McClure anyway. "Go start breakfast, Red." As McClure departed, hastening out into the chilly early dawn, the stranger opened his eyes again, and stared steadily up at Jason. He did not speak again, did not make any attempt to utter a sound, he just lay there studying Jason.

Howell got up and swore because he'd been kneeling so long he had a charley horse in one calf. He went hobbling away saying he had a clean shirt which he'd fetch back and they'd bandage the stranger's chest.

The stranger followed every move Jason made with his sunken, lusterless eyes, but he said nothing and made no attempt to lift a hand or move a leg. He looked better, now that he was conscious, but Jase had no illusions about that. Acute clarity not uncommonly arrived in an ailing person, one minute before darkness closed in forever.

He took the stranger's hat closer to the lamp and hunkered over there sifting through its contents, all the while with those sunken, feverish eyes unwaveringly upon him.

Dawn came fully, eventually, and Jase turned off the lamp. In that steely-wet light the wounded man looked worse than ever. Each deep crease in his face showed more harshly, and his beard stubbleadded to the evil shading of his strong features. Jase was sure, even without reading the cruelty and hardness below him on the ground, that what he had in his barn was an outlaw.

Right then he could accept that without any qualms. The man was two-thirds dead, that was what mattered first. At least Jason *thought* that was what mattered first.

36

CHAPTER SIX

THERE WERE CERTAIN THINGS THAT HAD TO BE DONE, so Jason left Red McClure with the wounded man while he and Mike Howell rode out.

They did not discuss the stranger very much, both of them refraining for the same reason: he would be dead for a fact when they got back about suppertime, and beyond that, what was there to speculate about? Except for the US-branded horse—and Jase had not mentioned this to either of his riders—there had been nothing very significant in the stranger's belongings. Of course, if folks *wanted* to speculate, the stranger would be a pretty fair topic. But rangemen were not like women; they never spoke just to use up a lot of fresh air.

Jase led the way up to the rolling, green foothills to make certain the cattle were not trying to drift back, and to make certain everything was as it should be otherwise.

It was. He and Mike Howell rode several miles to the west, then turned back and headed in the opposite direction. The cows were turning rich, dark red, which signified that they were layering up fat underneath. The little calves ran like scorpions, with their tails hooked over their backs, at the sight of horsemen, not actually all that terrified, but the horsemen were a wonderful excuse to run every which way.

They found a late-calving heifer and went to sit under a big shaggy old fir tree to watch her labors. She was not a very large animal, which could mean she'd have trouble. But she didn't; she was only down about five or six minutes rolling up on to her side and straining, when the calf came.

They got back astride and headed on eastward until they found a dead coyote. Jase recalled the yapping last night, but this coyote had been dead longer than that.

They were satisfied that the bushy-tailed little sharp-faced critter was dead, and thought perhaps that the coyote had allowed a horned cow to get too close. It happened, occasionally; a cow that any other time would run from a coyote, would turn back and fight when she had a calf.

Then they found the tracks of a shod horse cutting due southward across their route and halted to sit in silence, making an assessment for a few moments before Jase reined up northward.

"It's probably the stranger's sign," he told Mike. "We've got lots of time, let's mosey up there for a ways."

It was the stranger's sign all right. Mike found two places where the horse had paused, and each place was marked by dark splashes of blood on the leaves and grass.

They went a mile, until the foothills became slightly steeper, up-ended and brushy, then they stopped and gazed along the front of the immense cordillera, wondering which of many canyons he might have crossed down through. Mike suddenly said, "You know what just come to me, Boss? That feller *had* to know how bad he was hit when he braced the mountains on the far side. But he still attempted the crossing, which is somethin' even a right healthy man with a packhorse loaded with grub wouldn't do just for the hell of it."

Jase said, "What's your point?"

"He figured he'd die up in them mountains."

Jase considered that for a while. When they were ready to turn back all he said was, "Well, if that was it,

38

he sure picked a good way to do it."

They headed for home with a lowering, red sun off on their right side. Once, they spoke briefly about returning in a week with the wagon to set up camp in the foothills and start working the cattle. Mike asked where the marking grounds were and Jase told him. Then he reminisced for another mile or two about how he and his brother had learned, the hard way, about roping and cutting and heading and heeling when their father had been alive. Beyond that not a whole lot was said.

They arrived back at the ranch while dusk was falling. They rode the last half mile watching the buildings, particularly the log barn, and as they headed in Mike sighed and said, "Well, we'll be havin' our own special burying tomorrow," and Jason agreed with him in silence as he swung off out front, looped his reins and walked into the gloomy barn with ringing spurs, and with Mike about ten feet behind him.

The stranger wasn't dead.

Red had evidently fed the man because there was a plate on the ground nearby, and a coffee cup. Also, the pony of whisky, noticeably depleted, was lying in the straw and hay.

Red had removed the stranger's boots and had washed him. The man looked comfortable and he was conscious, but there was no mistaking his borderline condition, still.

His eyes wandered a little, turning aimlessly one way or the other, and his lips were as grey as bedrock. He was no longer bleeding, which was a good thing—unless of course he was bled out, and the only way they'd know that would be when he closed his eyes for the last time.

Otherwise he just might make it. But if he did, it

would be one hell of a long haul.

Jason pushed back his hat, hooked his thumbs, and said, "Anything new, Red?"

McClure was rolling a smoke when he answered. "No. He ate a little and I give him another couple shots of likker, but the coffee seemed to do the most good." McClure stuck the cigarette between his lips but did not light it—that was basic range etiquette: a man never lit up in the barn. "He ain't real talkative. He hears everything you say, and he understands, but he don't answer questions worth a damn."

Jase wasn't surprised. "He'll have his reasons, Red. Anyway, he's pretty weak, from the look of him."

McClure had evidently been worrying about something else. "We going to leave him in the barn overnight?"

Jase didn't have to ponder that very long. "That wound'll break open if we move him. He'll be all right here. Fetch some extra blankets and let's bundle him up."

Red left and Mike moved over to peer downwards. "How do you feel?" he called to the stranger, and did not get so much as a flicker of an eyelash to indicate he had been heard, so he turned towards Jase to speak again. "If he ain't dead by morning, Boss, he could hang on like this for months. I seen an old man up in Powder City one time, who got run over by a freighter, and he lasted out the whole blessed season, and only cashed in just before Christmas."

Jase was studying the stranger. The first surprise at finding him in the barn, and the second shock of seeing what condition the man was in, had passed. Now, Jason was thinking beyond; even if the stranger died, there were going to be a lot of questions to be answered. "In the morning," he said thoughtfully, "I'd better ride in for the sheriff. Whoever he is, he can't spend the whole summer out here like this."

Red returned and the three of them went to work creating a straw pallet which they got the stranger on to, then they trundled him into three blankets like a cocoon, and when he groaned Red reached for the pony of whisky, but Jase glared and Red left the bottle lying. Then the three of them went out to the doorway to confer. McClure's idea of remedial care involved keeping the stranger warm, still, and well fortified, while Mike was of the opinion that if an infection hadn't already started, it shortly would, and since the stranger was going to die anyway, they might as well make him comfortable. Jase agreed with both of them about keeping the man warm and still and well looked after. But he told McClure to use the whisky sparingly, and he told Mike that if, when he changed the bandage, it looked like there was an infection, they'd have to send down to Yellowstone, which was a long way off, for the only medical doctor Jase knew about, and at once Mike screwed up his face and said, "You know what somethin' like that could cost?"

Jason knew. "What else can we do—just let him lie there and die?"

"Get rid of him," said Howell. "He ain't rightly none of our responsibility anyway."

McClure, who had spent the day around the barn, came up with something. "He ain't got any money. He told me that much . . . And there's something he *didn't* tell me: That liver-chestnut he was riding has an army brand under the mane."

Jason saw Mike Howell faintly stiffen. "By gawd, a horse thief," exclaimed Mike, squirting it out so that all

41

the words ran together. He turned and looked back into the barn. "Maybe you got the right idea, Boss. Maybe you'd better get the sheriff out here in the morning." As he faced forward again, another thought hit Howell. "And it won't look very good for us fellers, if you don't fetch the law. Folks got a way of figuring men who know a horse thief can't be a whole lot better'n one."

Jason gazed at Mike with a fresh-dawning thought. If there was one thing he did *not* particularly need, it was for folks over in Junction to hear that he had been caring for a horse thief. He even remembered that little conversation he'd had with Tassie Meredith out front of the general store when he'd tried to convey to her his thoughts about being the brother of an outlaw. Now, that seemed more pertinent than ever.

"Wish to hell his horse had turned off in some other direction," he told his riders, and went walking over across the yard towards the main house.

Jason, who had been a quiet man and a thoughtful one even before the passing of his parents, and the notoriety of his brother, had left him pretty much alone on the range, had somehow managed to avoid the pitfall of many men possessing those related virtues— gloominess—but as he made supper that night and reconsidered his position, he almost got gloomy.

Anyone else could find a wounded man in his barn, and even if it turned out the man had been shot by the law, and even if it turned out that he was a horse thief riding a government issue mount, almost any other rancher would be viewed as the inadvertent principal in an affair that 'could have happened to anyone'. But not Jase Hurd, the brother of Frank Hurd, notorious gunman and outlaw who had left his mark all across the northwest for something like eight years, until they caught him and hanged him. If Frank Hurd's brother was found to be caring for an outlaw . . . He could almost hear them saying it: 'Well, I always knew the bad blood was in him too.' 'Good thing his folks didn't live to see *him* turn out bad like his brother.' 'Jason Hurd hiding a wounded horse thief? Well, naturally!'

After a light supper Jase mixed a drink of whisky and branch water and took it out on to the front porch to sit a spell, something he did quite often this time of year. Otherwise, the past few winters, he'd had his nightcap in front of the fireplace when there was icy wind howling around and maybe snow falling.

Tonight, the soaring old moon was plumb full and early rising, and of course the coyotes sounded north of the foothills, back up in the broken, brushy country not really influenced by the moon, as the Indians used to contend, but simply because a full moon made the land two-thirds as bright as day, and that made hunting a lot easier.

They'd be out, like a hang-mob, running in packs tonight. Jase sipped his nightcap and wondered where the wolf had gone. Due north beyond the cordillera it was said that in the past four of five years a lot of sheep-men had taken up land over there. If that wolf had a lick of sense he'd cross the mountains. Sheep wouldn't stand and fight like an old cow would, when they had young. A wolf could get as fat as a tick, living along the fringe of sheep country. Until someone shot him, of course.

Who had tried to kill that stranger, the army, the law, some cowman maybe, who saw the stranger trying to rope out a fresh horse from his corrals, or was it a fighting cowboy in some town beyond the mountains?

Jase finished his drink, set the glass resolutely aside, rose and walked down off the porch heading in the direction of the barn. He wanted some answers. Even if he had to prime the stranger with that pony of whisky, or what remained of it, and even if he had to shake him awake, he wanted some answers.

The bunkhouse was dark, all the buildings were silver-lined in the moonlight. Out beyond, where the range ran for miles, visibility was good enough to enable a man to see a fair distance.

Inside the barn, though, it was darkly gloomy. When Jason got close, he got a surprise. The stranger had somehow managed to unwrap his blankets. It looked as though he had actually been trying to get up.

He was lying there, weak as a kitten, his face shiny with sweat, looking upwards at big Jase Hurd.

CHAPTER SEVEN

JASON DROPPED TO ONE KNEE WITH A FROWN. "WHAT the hell are you trying to do?" he demanded of the wounded man.

He got an answer that was resolute, even though it was shaky. "What the hell does it—look like—I was tryin' to do? I heard—you fellers talking at the—doorway. You thought I'd passed—out. I was playin'—possum. I heard you say somethin' about—going—after—the—sheriff . . . Where's my—gun?"

Jase didn't bother with that question. It was incredible; that man was too weak to lift a hand, but he had struggled, had floundered around with a real effort to find his horse and escape. Jase picked up the pony and pulled the cork. "Two swallows," he said, and poured when the stranger tilted back his head. As he put the cork back and tossed the bottle aside in the hay, he

44

sighed and shook his head. "Mister, you got more grit than brains. Even if you could stand up, and even if you could get on your horse—or someone's horse, anyway—you'd never go a mile before you passed out and fell off, and maybe bled to death this time."

"Where's my—gun?"

Jason could not see the man's sunken eyes in the gloom, he could only make out his tough-set jaw and mouth. "It's over at the main house, where it's going to stay. You couldn't hold it up if I gave it to you."

The stranger was breathing in a fluttery way and lying strung out. Jase reached, pulled the three blankets back over the man, and said, "Relax, you're not going anywhere. What's your name?"

The dimly seen face remained closed and set like granite. Not a word issued from the thin, long-lipped mouth.

"Where are you from and where did you get that liver-chestnut gelding?"

The wounded man might as well have been dead.

Jason leaned above the man, his massive shoulders and chest filling the stranger's vision. "Listen to me, mister, I've got a hell of a lot more at stake in this mess than you know, and I'm going to get some answers out of you. Understand?"

"Go—to—hell!"

Something seemed to add strength to the wounded man. Maybe it was defiance and maybe it was indignation, or possibly both, but at least his words lost that hoarse, whispery sound and rang forth in the dark hush of the barn.

Jason smiled downward. "Who shot you, the army for stealing their horse, or the law?"

The stranger's tongue made a darting circuit of the

45

stranger's cracked, peeling lips. He looked upwards straight into Jason's eyes without flinching, and said nothing.

Jase lay a hand upon the man's shoulder and slowly closed his fingers. "I meant it, mister, when I said I'm going to get some answers out of you." He tightened his grip and gave the stranger a gentle shake. "Who shot you?"

". . . Leave me be, you bastard."

Jason loosened his hold a little. "Who shot you?"

"Some gawddamned jehu inside—when I tried to stop —the stage—back up north—somewhere. I never seen the lousy—gun—when he fired from—inside. It was worse than gettin'—branded with a red-hot—iron."

"How long ago?"

The stranger's tongue made its darting circuit again. "How long ago? I don't know. I run for it—and got into the mountains—and kept bearing—southward. How long I been lying here?"

Jason reached for the pony and gave the outlaw another two swallows. Red McClure's 'medicine' seemed to make this a lot easier, whether it was good for the injured man or not, and right at this moment Jase didn't give a damn about that.

He was shielding not only a horse thief, but a stage robber and a fugitive as well. Even Frank had never stolen a horse nor robbed a stage.

"What's your name?" he asked again.

The stranger's sweaty face looked as dark as old leather in the barn gloom when he said, "William Smith; what's your name?"

"Jason Hurd. I own the ranch you rode down over to reach this barn."

The outlaw moved his head slightly. "Hurd? Any

46

relation to—Frank Hurd?"

Jase felt like swearing or biting his tongue. Instead he asked another question. "What is your real name? This time try the truth."

But the outlaw was watching Jase from slitted eyes now, and whatever his anguish and defiance had made him say and do before, that was all changed now. "I can't see you real good in here—but before—when it was daylight . . . by gawd, you *do* resemble Frank a little." The outlaw weakly wobbled his head. "By gawd, I deserved this—kind of luck."

Jason said, "I'll tell you what kind of luck you're going to have. In the morning I'll fetch back the sheriff, and after that you belong to him."

The outlaw breathed shallowly for a moment before attempting to speak again. "Yeah? Then you can square that with Elsie, can't you?"

Jase looked at the man. He did not look as good now as he'd looked before that last jolt of whisky. He hadn't made any sense either, so Jase got heavily up to his full height and considered going on back to the house to bed.

"I asted you," exclaimed the wounded man. "How you goin' to square it with Elsie? I'm her brother. Didn't you know that? Didn't Frank write you—that?"

Something just beyond Jason's reach seemed to make some kind of sense. "Tell me what?" he replied. "I only saw Frank once, at my mother's funeral, out of those bad years of his. What should he have told me?"

"Elsie," stated the outlaw. "Elsie's my sister . . . she's the one Frank had Donnie by. Now then—how you goin' to square it with Elsie—that you handed over her brother?"

Jason reached out a thick arm to the stall wall. "Who

is Donnie?"

"Gawddamn but you're—ignorant. Donnie's Frank's boy out of Elsie. You dumb bas—"

"You lousy liar," spat Jason.

The outlaw panted and said nothing for a while, but he could make out Jason's face, evidently, because he very weakly wobbled his head back and forth. "Not lyin'," he muttered.

Jason stepped away, turned and went up towards the front of the barn. He *had* to be lying. Frank wouldn't have done that; if there'd been a woman and a little boy, Frank wouldn't have gone on the way he'd done, until they caught and hanged him.

Jase swung and returned to the wounded man's side. He leaned and caught the outlaw in a fierce grip. "You lie to me," he said very softly, "and you're not going to last until morning. One more lie, mister, and I'll kill you while you're lying right there on your back . . . What is your name?"

The reply came faintly. "Houston Hickman."

"That was a lousy lie about Frank Hurd and your sister, wasn't it?"

". . . Truth, so help me."

"Where are they now—your sister and the little boy?"

"In Cheyenne . . . Where's that—whisky? Hurry . . ."

Jason did not move for a long time, but eventually he knelt, groped for the bottle in the straw, pulled the cork and hoisted the outlaw's head.

The man was dead.

Jase eased him back down, put aside the bottle and knelt there looking into the malevolent, lined face; it looked no less malignant, strong and cruel in death than it had looked in life, and that was unusual, Jason thought; most of the dead people he had seen had turned out to look different in a gentle, kind of resigned and relaxed manner. Maybe it was the poor light.

He got heavily upright and walked out of the barn. Over at the porch he happened to catch sight of his empty glass, so he scooped it up and went on inside, out to the pantry, and made himself a second, even stronger, mixture of whisky and branch water. He took this with him to the bedroom, and while he wearily got ready for bed, he paused now and then to sip. By the time the glass was empty he was ready for sleep.

He probably shouldn't have slept, but it was worry, not conscience, that troubled him. The whisky no doubt helped a lot.

When he opened his eyes again it was almost daylight beyond the windows. He rose and got ready for the new day. By the time Mike and Red appeared on the front porch Jase had had his coffee and side-meat and was ready. He knew what they were going to tell him.

"That feller took off in the night," said Howell. "He's out there now, stiffer'n a ramrod. Want us to hitch the buckboard?"

Jason nodded. "I'll be along directly. Wrap him in a couple of blankets and lay him out in the rig." Jason went back inside to get the outlaw's hat, with his personal effects still in it; a Barlow clasp knife, a broken comb, some money—about sixty dollars all told, paper and silver—a soiled bandanna, some Durham tobacco and a little steel shaving mirror.

Not a hell of a lot for a man to own after he'd been through life for about thirty years.

Jase went outside wearing his hat and gun belt, but not his spurs. He toyed with the idea of sending Mike or Red into town with the corpse, but that wouldn't change anything; Beau would ride out to talk to him anyway.

49

He went out and watched his riders boost the body over the low side and place it in back, then he said, "Start shoeing the horses while I'm gone. I'll fetch back some supplies. You boys low on anything in the bunkhouse?"

"Coffee and baking powder," said Mike Howell. "What should we do with that US branded horse? It won't look good if a squad of soldiers comes ridin' in and sees him here."

"Leave him be and see that he's got plenty of feed and water," replied Jason, evening up the lines and kicking off the brake. "I ought to be back early." He flicked the lines, the team threw weight into their collars, and Jason drove out of the yard leaving Red and Mike looking after him.

Red said, "That's a pretty fair saddle in the barn, Mike, and that hurt feller'll never have no use for it again."

Howell looked down his peeling nose at McClure. "Yeah? An' suppose you're out on the range ridin' that saddle someday, redskin, and a bunch of fellers lopes up and pitches a lariat over a low limb and cuts your breath off for riding a stoled saddle?"

"They don't hang folks for stealing *saddles*," protested the 'breed, "and, anyway, I wouldn't have stoled it."

Mike made a bitter little smile. "You care to chance it, redskin?"

McClure decided the saddle wasn't *that* good, and led the way over towards the shoeing shed, where he and Mike lined out the tools, stoked up the forge, rummaged for a couple of those traditional muleskin aprons, then one of them, McClure, strode across the yard to fetch back the first few horses.

50

The day was not too hot, which was favorable. If there was one thing that sapped all the git-up-and-go out of a man shoeing horses, it was a blistering spell of hot weather.

When McClure returned and led one horse inside, leaving three others tied to the rack out front, Mike, shirt peeled off, underwear sleeves pushed up above his elbows, eyed the splayed, winter-ruined feet of the horse and said, "Sure as hell that feller was an outlaw, Red. Now I'm sort of wonderin'—could there be maybe a couple hunnert dollars reward on his scalp?"

McClure was stopped in his tracks by this stunning and magnificent prospect. "By golly, you might be right. Who'd get it?"

"Me, damn it," snapped Mike Howell indignantly. "I'm the one routed out of bed when I heard horses squealing, and found him, ain't I ?"

"Yes. But I found him second, and that means I'm entitled to something, don't it?"

Howell became magnanimous. "Sure. You can have a third of it."

McClure got mad. "A *third,* damn you anyway, I'm entitled to *half* of it."

Howell refused to budge, refused to arbitrate this at all. With a thick rasp in one brawny hand he used it for a pointer. "Commence heating a set of shoes and quit standing around, will you?"

CHAPTER EIGHT

BEAU SAT AT HIS DESK AND LISTENED TO EVERYTHING Jason said—which was not *all* of it, but the rest was personal—and when Jason was finished Beau leaned

51

back and considered the fly-specked ceiling.

"That's not all Hickman did," he exclaimed. "I got a flyer on him three days back." Beau paused, then said, "He was a running mate of Frank's, Jase. They caught an express messenger down in Denver and cleaned him out of six thousand dollars." Beau paused again, not wanting to meet Jase's glance. "They killed him. That's what the law was hunting Frank for when he got careless down in Arizona." Beau rocked forward and leaned on the desk. "Tell me something: How did Hickman happen to come to you?"

Jase answered woodenly. "I told you; he said that after getting shot he rode into the mountains and just kept riding."

"Frank never mentioned him to you?"

"No. And if I hadn't told Hickman my name he wouldn't have known Frank and I were brothers."

Beau said, "Well, I'll keep him in the horse shed until they dig a hole at the cemetery." He raised up a little and searched among the clutter on top of the desk until he found the flyer. "Five hundred dollar reward, Jase."

For five seconds Jason sat perfectly still, then he said, "Beau, do you know what you can do with that five hundred dollars?" and stamped up to his full height out of the chair and slammed out of the office.

Beau sat like stone, looking at the door. He put down the poster, reached for his hat and rose to go after Jason, but when he got outside Jase was nowhere in sight. His rig was out back where they'd unloaded the body, so Beau hurried around there. Jason was not with the rig, it still stood in the shed shade, the horses pleasantly drowsing.

Beau gave it up and returned to his office to write the official letter of notification to the authorities down in

52

Denver who had posted the reward for Houston Hickman.

Jason was standing out front of the stage depot when Tassie drove by in her topbuggy, heading north. She hauled up in surprise at sight of him. "Jason . . . ? I was just on my way out to the ranch. I didn't know you were in town."

Without speaking he walked out to her and leaned on the rig. "I was going to hunt you up after a while, and see if you'd want to talk to me, Tassie."

Her grey gaze clouded a little. "If I'd want to talk to you . . . ? What is it, Jason?" She moved a little. "Get in. We'll drive up the road a mile or so." When he leaned, looking in at her without moving, she said it again, "Get in."

He obeyed, and the light springs sagged perilously from his weight, then she clucked and her horse started off again. They were several hundred yards beyond town before she spoke again.

"Is something wrong?"

He leaned back as he answered. "Yeah. And it's a mess. I just bought a passage on the stage to Cheyenne."

She slowed the horse and turned her head. "Start at the beginning, Jason."

He had to grope through to find an actual beginning. He also had to decide whether—as he'd been thinking back there out front of the stage depot—whether she was the one to talk to, or whether there was really *anyone* to talk to.

She pulled the rig off the road and drove into a clump of pale-trunked little delicate aspen trees where the shade was soft and welcome, then she set the footbrake, looped the lines and turned very purposefully towards him.

"Jaso—what *is* it?"

He told her, beginning with the arrival of the wounded man at his barn. She did not say a word throughout his entire recitation. Even after he had finished, she still sat like stone.

He climbed out of the buggy, strolled up and removed the check-rein so the horse could drop its head and crop grass, then he leaned on the animal, looking back at her.

She said, "Do you believe it?"

He answered that obliquely. "Well, that's why I bought the ticket to Cheyenne. To go up there and see if there is a little boy named Donnie." He stepped away from the horse, deeper into the aspen grove, deeper into the shade, and said, "I hope there isn't. That's what I kept thinking on the drive into town this morning. I hope that dead man was lying."

"Jason, you don't sound like you think he was lying."

He had no answer to that.

She got out of the rig too, and walked into the shade with him. She was not a small woman, but in front of him she seemed quite small. "If you find there *is* a little boy, Jason . . . ?"

He'd had no trouble coming to grips with that, on the drive to town. "I'll fetch him back with me."

"What about—Elsie?"

"I don't know," he said. He hadn't really thought much about Elsie; hadn't allowed her to get past the block in his mind.

"But she's his mother. You can't just go up there and take the little boy and bring him back down here." Tassie turned abruptly with her back to Jase. "It's true. I can *feel* how true it is."

Jase, who was not a hating man, looked at her from the back and came very close to despising his dead

54

brother. What could this Elsie be in comparison to Tassie Meredith? Of all the damned stupid fools in the world, Frank had to be right up there close to the front row.

She walked off a short distance, still keeping her head averted. Eventually, when the silence was becoming intolerable, she said, "*I'll* go up there, Jason. This time of year you're busy, so I'll go to Cheyenne and see if it is true."

He balked at that. "It's not your problem, Tassie. At least—this part of Frank's life isn't your problem. No. I'll go up there and—"

"But suppose there is no little boy? I can go up and at least make certain, one way or the other, Jason, and that way it won't be a wasted trip for you. Aren't you getting ready to work the cattle?"

"In a week, maybe," he replied, watching her face in the soft-shadowed sunlight. "I can spare a few days, and it's not that big a trip."

She said, "Will you promise me that you won't just take the little boy, Jason, and come home with him?"

He hadn't thought much about that, either. It had seemed natural, during the course of his troubled thinking on the drive to town, to envisage bringing Frank's son back to the ranch with him. Well, the stage wouldn't leave for Cheyenne until morning, so he had an entire day to iron out the wrinkles in his thinking. But he wasn't going to make any promises when he had no idea what he might run into up at Cheyenne, so he said, "Frank's still managing to reach out and stir trouble up for you and me, Tassie. I probably shouldn't have told you any of this."

"How long do you suppose it would have been before I found out?" she demanded, moving back closer to him

55

in among the aspens, her eyes nearly black with emotional turmoil.

He did not believe she ever would have learned about the other woman and the child. At least, if she ever *did* hear about it, it would be only rumor, and probably that wouldn't reach down to Junction for many years. Grudgingly, then, he decided that she *would* have found out someday. How those things happened he did not know, but they happened. Especially around Junction. Especially where Frank was concerned.

He savagely said, "Gawddamn Frank, anyway," and went back over where the horse was gorging on grass.

She came along, more slowly and without the same flash of temper. She seemed to have completely recovered from the shock and agitation by the time she joined him near the buggy.

"Jason?"

"Yes?"

"You didn't promise."

He turned to face her. "Don't hobble me, Tassie. How do I know what I'll run into up there?"

She let the subject drop. "I'll take you back to town, and you can get on home, and later this evening I'll drive out after we've both had more time to think. Is that all right?"

He said, "Yes," and hauled the horse's head up, hooked the check-rein, then handed Tassie back up into the rig and went around behind to get in on the opposite side. He had nothing more to say as they got back to the road and turned towards town.

She drove down the alleyway behind her father's building, where she kept her horse and rig, and there he left her, went up between two structures to Main Street and kept on going until he was in the alleyway out behind the jailhouse. There, he was untying his team when Beau came strolling along and said, "I was just shooting the bull with the stage agent, Jase. He told me you'd bought a seat on the morning coach for Cheyenne."

Jason climbed up to the buckboard's seat and showed a little of the annoyance he couldn't help but feel.

"What difference does that make to you, Beau?"

The sheriff leaned on the back wall of his jailhouse. "I don't rightly know," he said quietly, studying Jason's troubled face. "But look at it from my side of the road: You bring in a dead outlaw this morning, then you go buy stage passage up to Cheyenne, which was this outlaw's stamping ground, an hour later." Beau hesitated and looked from Jason to his burly harness horses. "Jason, is there something you left out?"

Instead of answering, Jase snapped the lines, braced when the horses hit their collars, and drove up through the alleyway to its end, then swung right heading for Main Street, which became the overland stage road beyond town northward.

Beau turned and walked on around front, stepped into the dust and went on a diagonal course up towards Archer Grant's telegraph office.

For Jason, the drive back home was worse than the drive to town a couple of hours earlier. The more he thought about it, the more he regretted confiding in Tassie.

But she had seemed the most reasonable person to talk to, and although he had never been a man who could not keep his own confidence, this time it had just come too startlingly, too suddenly and totally unexpectedly, and he'd felt a powerful urge to talk. Not to Beau, although he might have told Beau the whole story if there hadn't been Tassie, except that the kind of

57

tale he'd have had to tell the sheriff was the kind that embarrassed a man like Jase very much.

One thing was dead certain. There *was* a little boy. He knew it was true in the same way that Tassie had known it was true; by instinct.

As for Houston Hickman, back there in Beau's horse shed, Jason hardly thought about him at all until he got back to the ranch and his two sweating cowboys came forth from the shoeing shed to ask him point blank if there was a reward.

He sat and stared for a moment, then he nodded and climbed down. "Yeah. Five-hundred dollars. Why?"

Red became concerned about a little scratch on his hand, and Mike Howell's Adams apple bobbed a few times before he said, "Well, Red and me was figuring . . . I found that feller first, in the barn, Boss, and Red come in a few minutes later, so we was wondering . . ."

Jason understood, finally. "All right. The next time I see Sheriff Beaufort I'll put you boys in for it." He handed the lines to McClure. "Put up the rig and look after the horses, will you, Red?"

McClure's interest in his scratched hand evaporated in a second. "Be right happy to," he exclaimed, and led the team away.

Jase went on up to the main house, shed his town coat, got into his work boots, stood a moment in the cool parlor, then gave his head a troubled shake like a tormented bull in fly-time, and went back outside to help with the shoeing.

He would have to tell Mike and Red he'd be gone for a few days, up in Cheyenne, but they could handle anything that came up in his absence. Maybe, when he got back, they'd have a mascot to take out to the working grounds with them.

CHAPTER NINE

IT WAS DOUBTFUL IF MIKE AND RED KNEW ANYONE
had arrived at the ranch. They had put in a hard day at
shoeing, which was an occupation that wore down the
strongest of men. They had taken their soap and towels,
had gone over to the creek which ran northwest of the
yard, and after washing away the sweat and dirt, had
returned to make supper, and by then it was well past
sundown.

Usually, they played a few hands of blackjack before
retiring, but sometimes they just doused the lantern and
turned in.

Jase saw their light go out while he was eating
supper, and afterwards, while he was washing the
dishes, because it was his nature to recapitulate the
day's doings, he understood their weariness.

He felt weary, too, but in a different way and from a
different cause. He did not particularly want to go
through the house dusting and setting things to rights—
he was not a good housekeeper and did not care for the
chore, but it had to be done, particularly tonight when a
woman would be arriving.

By the time Tassie drove up out front he had the place
looking tolerably respectable. He left her waiting on the
porch while he took her rig to the barn, unhooked the
horse and made him comfortable in a stall, and on the
walk back across the dark yard he saw the moon casting
its strange brilliance ahead of it as it began to ascend, an
hour later tonight, from beyond some dark-standing
distant mountains.

She watched him return and when he reached the

59

steps she said, "I used to think full moon nights were especially wonderful," and smiled at him in the darkness of the overhanging porch roof.

He opened the door for her to enter first, thinking that full moon nights should be wonderful. Particularly to someone like Tassie Meredith. That was the kind of person full moon nights were made for.

Inside, with the lamps glowing and the tabletops glistening from their recent dusting, he went and poked at the little fire he'd made, then turned as she sat on the sofa over near the window overlooking the yard. She was a beautiful woman. Despite everything, there was a kind of mature serenity, a kind of mature acceptance, that set her apart from most of the women he had known.

She smiled at him. "Jason, something I learned long ago is that no matter how awful something seems at first, in time it shrinks down to normal size, and fits in with everything else." Her smile at him lingered, soft and sweet. "I'm not making excuses for Frank; what I'm saying is that this has *happened,* and regardless of how it upset us both earlier today, by now, tonight, it's begun to assume its actual size."

He accepted that because he, too, had thought about little else since arriving back home from town. But it was still a hard thing for him to live with, so he said, "Tassie, Frank's done enough to you and me. When we buried him that should have been the end of it. At least that should have been the end of his ability to do any more to us. That's how I felt at the funeral, and afterwards. We could live with the memory, because we had to. But gawddammit, now he's gone and reached out again, and this time it's not something that will go away with time, is it? This time it's a living damned

60

responsibility."

She looked into the fire. "Maybe not, Jason. Maybe Elsie is capable of handling it."

He wanted to snort disdainfully. He did not have her altruism. He was a man, but more, he was a man who had lived close to nature all his life, he knew that nature was entirely indifferent about a lot of things that people thought should be better, should be good. That dead outlaw had been the product, or the result, of an environment that did not produce a whole lot of virtuous people. He had already envisaged the dead outlaw's sister as some kind of feminine extenuation of her brother.

But he was careful about expressing his cynicism. All he said was: "Time will tell, Tassie. I'll be in Cheyenne in a day or two. She shouldn't be hard to find."

Her grey eyes lifted. "And if the little boy loves his mother, Jason . . . ?"

She was cornering him and he felt it. "What's best," he countered, "a boy growing up believing someone is special, when they aren't special except to him, or a boy growing up believing in decent things?"

"So you're really going up there to judge Elsie, Jason."

"No, I'm really going up there to see if Frank's son has even half a chance to grow up into something different than his father was." This was a modification of Jase's earlier feelings, but he had had most of the day to separate emotion from hard fact. "I kept thinking about what you said about the boy's mother. I *want* to believe she'll be different from what I expect her to be. If she is, I'll get right back on the stage and come home without ever speaking to either of them."

Tassie leaned, both hands clasped, and said, "Jason,

61

please let me do it." She put power into those few words. She did not press him nor elaborate, but he felt the force of her urgent appeal.

There was no *real* reason why she couldn't go, when he became detached enough from personal resolve to consider it, except that, being a man whose entire mature lifetime had been spent relying exclusively upon himself, in even matters of trivial concern, he felt himself to be better qualified.

"As a woman," she said, "let me go up there, see them, form a woman's opinion, then come back to you." She rose and walked over to him, in front of the fireplace. "Jason, do you know what's left—just you and me—and we *both* need the same satisfaction about this child. Except for . . . something in Frank . . . he could have been my child. Don't I deserve the right to at least see him?"

He raised a hand and gently brushed her cheek. Then he smiled. "Sure, you have a lot of rights, Tassie." The hand dropped back to his side. "My idea was to see them without them seeing me. At least until I was satisfied whether or not the boy needed me. If you ride right up and brace them, aren't either of them going to act very natural, are they?"

She agreed. "I'll be tactful." She held out her hand. "Your stage ticket."

He rummaged for it, handed it to her, and said, "How about a cup of coffee?" She agreed, so they went out to the kitchen, and the air out there was fresher, less troubled and hard to breathe.

As he worked firing up the stove, she watched with amused eyes. Frank hadn't been as large, as thick and massive as Jason was. Frank had possessed grace and Jason was lacking in lightness. Frank had been the kind of man who could feint when life turned on him; Jason was one of those men who did not take a backward step, even from life. It was hard, actually, to see much of Frank in his younger brother, except, perhaps, up around the eyes, and maybe a little in the curve of jaw and breadth of mouth.

He caught her smiling and said, "Well, I can't cook very well, but I know how to make coffee." He laughed a little self-consciously. "I used to have an Indian woman who came in a day or two each month and slicked the place up. But she got married to some feller and they went over to Idaho, around Fort Hall, to open a boardinghouse."

She said, "Jason, don't you eat with your riders?"

He didn't, and he never had for a very simple reason. As he told her, "Tassie, when you're with a couple of fellers from sunup until sundown, the biggest blessing for all of you is not to have to look at one another until the following morning." He finished with the fire and went to fill the pot with water from his bucket on the back porch, then he returned and put in ground coffee and set the pot on top of a burner lid.

She sat at the kitchen table, her red-rusty hair shining from lamp glow, her muscular, large upper body in its dark dress making a solid, powerful impression upon him as he leaned and regarded her from over by the stove.

It was a strange, rather uncomfortable little moment and although he sought for a way to abrogate it, he was temporarily tongue tied. She was up to it; in fact Tassie could sense things in people, as she now sensed Jason's discomfort, and his masculine thoughts.

"Let's suppose Frank's son can come here, Jason; aren't little boys who have been with their mothers

63

liable to be scarred worse by being put down in a man's world and made to adjust to that?"

He knew practically nothing of little children, boys or girls, and he did not want to get trapped into a discussion where he'd be in over his head, so he tried skirting around it by saying, "You knew his father, Tassie, and I knew both his father and his uncle—the feller who got shot trying to stop a stage. Seems to me he could learn the cow business here, and there'd always be enough to keep him too busy for a lot of brooding. Anyway, I hope I'm wrong, but I've got a feeling coming here may darned well be the lesser of two evils."

Out of the blue she said, "Jason, you need a wife."

It was like having someone pitch a bucketful of cold water over him. ". . . A wife?"

She smiled up at him. "Well, don't you? If he comes here you've got to remember, he can't be more than eight years old at the most, and more likely he's younger by a year or two." Tassie's grey gaze drifted to the massive black stove. "Are you going to give him coffee and fried steak for breakfast, and keep him in the saddle all day?"

Jason could see a world of difference between hiring a housekeeper and getting married. He'd had a housekeeper, of sorts, so he understood something about that, but he had never even casually considered getting married. There hadn't been time; first, it was Frank, and the stigma of being his brother, then his parents had begun to fail, and he'd had to take complete charge of the ranch.

Tassie said, "The coffee's boiling, Jason," and rose to go take the pot off the burner while he went to a shelf for cups and saucers.

It was good coffee; strong enough to keep a man going half a day. They sat at the table to drink it and although Tassie, who was an exceptionally good cook, weakened hers with tinned milk and sugar, before pronouncing it drinkable, Jase was rather proud of it. Not all his coffee turned out this strong and muscular. He told her of a rider he'd once employed, some years back while his father had still been alive, who'd had some tomfool notion that coffee should never be boiled longer than five minutes.

"Why, hell," he exclaimed, "anyone knows the longer you boil it the better it gets."

She smiled at him. "You must have cast iron insides, Jason. When I get back, maybe someday I could ride out and move the cattle with you, the way I used to when . . ."

"Yeah," he said, finishing it for her. "When Frank was around. Well, sure; come any time." He kept looking at her, then he grinned a little. "I reckon I was about sixteen . . ."

"And?"

"Well, you came out one time and we rode out, Frank, you, paw and me, and that feller used to hire on every summer named Wishbone—I don't know whatever became of him; after paw died he never came back. Anyway, I remember one day in particular. We were bringing the cattle down from the foothills. You and Frank rode up on top of a low little knoll, and I reckon it was the way the sun was standing, but when I saw you up there, with your hair down and sittin' straight up in the saddle, easy-like . . ." Jason reached for the coffee cup. He hadn't meant to get this carried away with his memories, but when he finished drinking she was still sitting across from him, her grey eyes dark, her perfect features relaxed and gentle, waiting. He put

65

the cup down.

"I promised myself that someday, somewhere, I'd find me a girl just like you."

Jason got up abruptly to go refill his cup. From the stove he said, "Care for some more?"

She replied softly, "No thanks. I've got to get back." When he turned, she was also standing. They looked steadily at one another, then she turned, and he followed her on through and out on to the porch where moonlight made the night half as brilliant as day.

They went slowly, side by side, down to the barn, saying nothing. He got her horse, tossed on the harness, hauled up the rig and buckled the shafts into place, then turned the outfit so it would be facing the proper direction, and when he went back to help her into the buggy, she climbed up swiftly without touching his offered hand, and reached for the lines without looking at him. But just before leaving she looked down and said, "I'm glad I came out, Jase, and soon as I get back I'll come out again."

He nodded, stepped clear, and half-raised a hand as she drove away. Because of the moonlight he could see her for almost a mile after she left the yard.

CHAPTER TEN

THE DAY WHEN HE HAD EXPECTED TO BE ON THE STAGE bound for Cheyenne, he was instead four miles from the home place with Red and Mike hauling some deadfalls to the marking grounds in the ranch wagon. They had this kind of work to do every late spring or early summer before drifting the cattle down to be worked. The wood was for branding fires.

66

There were two corrals, neither of them very large, for 'doctoring' and general use, sometimes for keeping their horses handy and confined while all three men worked between the fire and the bare patch where the cutting, ear-marking, and branding was done. There was nothing easy about being at a working ground, unless it was, as today, the business of getting ready.

They spent almost the entire day out there, then piled into the wagon and headed for home a couple of hours ahead of sunset. Jase wasn't very talkative, but then, he was never loquacious, so throughout the day there hadn't been a lot of conversation. The only time they discussed the dead outlaw was on the way out, when Red McClure pointed to the freshly shod remuda and said, "Maybe we should've tied that gelding to the tailgate when you took Hickman into town."

Mike squinted, then snorted. "Quit worrying, Red, he'll be all right for a few days. Anyway, if the army comes along they aren't likely to figure we're trying to keep their consarned horse, if we got him running loose like that."

Jase agreed with Red. "I forgot about him, but Red's right, I should have trailed him and handed him over to Sheriff Beaufort." He gazed at the horse as they drove past. "That's one hell of a fine animal."

"A case of the horse bein' more worthwhile than the man ridin' him," opined Howell, and this thought seemed to somehow prompt another thought, that was not very closely related at all. "Five hunnert dollars, Boss. With my share of that kind of money, I just may not go out lookin' for work next summer."

McClure said, "The hell you won't. By next summer it'll all be spent and you know it."

Howell laughed and even Jase smiled. It was the

67

truth.

They worked hard, said little, and got back to the ranch with plenty of daylight left. Red and Mike loafed and Jase went over to the canvas-topped working wagon to rummage in the chuck-box tailgate for the list that had been kept there over the years; it gave the exact supplies a four-man team would require for the three or four days they would be at the working ground. The list had been made by Jase's father about ten years back, and it had been compiled as the result of almost a half-century of experience.

Most of the items, like flour and coffee and baking powder, were already in the storeroom off the back of the main house. An indication that times had changed lay in the notation in Joseph Hurd's handwriting, that a rider was to be sent to the mountains with a packhorse two or three days early to bring back some elk or deer meat. Now, Jase carved off a quarter of the beef kept in the well house, instead of sending anyone into the mountains to hunt.

When he was finishing with this job, was satisfied in his mind that they probably had enough of everything without having to go into town with the buckboard, his attention was caught by a high, rolling call from out over the range.

He saw the rider raise his arm overhead in the old-time manner of signifying friendly intentions, about the same time Red and Mike came tumbling forth from their game of blackjack at the bunkhouse in response to that same call.

It took a little while to figure out who the rider was. Although the air was as clear as glass, and it was possible to make things out for several miles, actual identification took longer. It was Jedediah Beaufort. By the time he got to the yard Red and Mike had decided he hadn't come to see them, especially, and had disappeared back inside the bunkhouse, but Jase had no illusions; eventually, before Beau left, Red and Mike would find some excuse to mention the matter of the Hickman reward.

Beau turned and rode over where Jase was leaning upon the canvas-topped wagon. Having been a range rider himself, Beau swung down as he said, "Getting ready to go out to the working grounds, Jase? You know, sometimes, when I get to thinking back . . ." Beau let it die and looped his reins round the front wagon wheel. "You can't ask for better weather than this," he said, looking out and around, as though he hadn't almost mentioned something that would have been painful for them both. Then he became brisk. "Didn't see you get on the stage this morning and thought maybe you'd been taken sick or something."

Jase smiled a little. "Like hell you did."

Beau smiled back the same way, thinly. "All right. I saw Tabitha Meredith get on in your place." Beau fished forth his Durham sack and went to work on a cigarette. "Howard wasn't much help. All he'd tell me was that she decided, sometime between yesterday and this morning, to ride up to Cheyenne." As Beau shoved the sack and papers back into his shirt pocket, a crumpled little yellow slip of paper, the kind Archer Grant inscribed his telegraph messages on, showed briefly. Beau blew smoke and regarded Jase thoughtfully. "You're not very talkative this morning," he said.

Jase never was very talkative, unless he had something to say. Right now, he would rather just listen. "Like you said, Beau, it's a nice day."

The sheriff inhaled, exhaled, and his face got a tough

69

set to it. "Why in the hell do you have to go and make this so hard for both of us?" he demanded of Jason. "Tassie didn't just up and decide to go have a look at the town of Cheyenne."

"Did you talk to her?" asked Jase.

Beau fished for that slip of yellow paper. "Nope. Never said a word to her." He got the paper and unfolded it. "Houston Hickman, one sister, two brothers, reside in this city," he read. "Sister and child came here from Denver two years ago. Sister's name is Elsa Hickman. It is thought she lived in Denver and other places with Frank Hurd. No reward on brothers, but both have been in trouble with the law."

Beau slowly folded the paper and pocketed it. He smoked a moment, then said, "It's the kid, isn't it, Jase?"

There was no point in lying. "Yeah, it's Frank's kid. That's what Hickman told me just before he died."

Beau had evidently been doing his share of thinking, too, on the ride out from town. "Well, providing you didn't send Tassie into some kind of damned trouble, Jase, maybe it's better she went than you."

Jase frowned. "What kind of trouble?"

"How would I know?" replied Beau. "You heard what the telegram said: Hickman has two brothers and they've both been in trouble with the law . . . Tassie wasn't figuring on trying to catch the child and bring it back with her, was she? Because that, I think, could cause a heap of trouble for her—for all of us, in fact."

"No," muttered Jase, "she's just going to see—well—if he needs something. If he's getting along all right."

Beau dropped his smoke and ground it out under a boot toe. "Yeah. I figured out what I think you got in mind, while I was riding out this evening, and I think

70

you're probably right; Frank's boy'd be a sight better off with you, down here, than with three more Hickmans up there."

Jason saw Red and Mike emerge across the yard, and that reminded him of something. "About that reward," he said, watching the two cowboys trying to decide whether to cross the yard or not, "McClure and Howell, my pair of riders, got it coming, Beau."

The sheriff took that in stride. "All right. I'll need statements from them. There shouldn't be any hitch. Send them in some day." Beau fished out his watch and squinted at it. "Be time for supper when I get back," he said, tucking away the watch. "Jase, if you'd told me yesterday, I could have telegraphed up to Cheyenne and got the information for you." He turned to tug loose his reins.

Jase knew an explanation was in order, but all he could force himself to say was: "It's a personal thing, Beau. Folks'll probably be talking about me having that outlaw in my barn as it is . . . By the way, he was riding a right fine liver-chestnut with an army brand on its neck. We turned it out with the ranch horses, but maybe you'd better take it back with you, just in case the army comes around."

Beau swung up and shook his head. "Not this evening. I'll come by for it some other time. Or, if you're coming into town, maybe you could bring the horse with you." Beau nodded, and regarded Jason for a moment before saying, "Do us both a favor, will you? Next time, tell me the whole confounded story, Jase." He did not await an answer, but reined around and got a fair start before Mike Howell and McClure started swiftly across the yard.

Jason intercepted them by the canvas-topped wagon.

"He said he'd put you in for the money, but you'll have to go into town one of these days and give him the full story."

Howell looked after Sheriff Beaufort, then nodded his head, quite satisfied. "We'll do that, one of these days when the work's slack and before we go out to the working grounds."

Jason squinted upward. Daylight was fast ending, finally. He wondered where Tassie would be tonight. There were a number of fair sized towns between Junction, Colorado, and Cheyenne, in southern Wyoming. She'd be all right.

It probably would have been better, too, if he'd told Beau the whole story. Well, now he knew, so that at least resolved the issue that had made him ride out to the ranch.

McClure and Howell were heading towards the barn to pitch feed to the three stalled horses down there. It was the rule on a cow outfit to always keep a couple of saddle mounts handy, but no more, unless there was work to be done the following day, because putting up hay was something cowmen simply did not do, unless they absolutely had to. They'd rather buy it already hauled and in their barns from some homesteading sod-buster.

Jase headed in the direction of the house and got midway across the yard before the distant, flat, shockwave of sound reverberated. He stopped in his tracks and whirled. Over at the barn Mike and Red sprang forth from the shadows. There was no mistaking the muzzle blast of a carbine, even when there was no reason to expect to hear it.

Jase twisted and called backwards. "Get saddled!" He ran to the house for his shellbelt, then ran back to the

72

barn where Mike and Red were working feverishly. As Jase took over the bridling, his men went in a lope to the bunkhouse; when they emerged both were carrying carbines too.

There had only been that one shot, but Jase knew his range, knew about where that gunshot had sounded from. It had been on the same course Beau had taken on his way back to town.

It didn't make a lick of sense to Jase, but he rode with his eyes narrowed and probing up ahead. He remembered that Beau hadn't had a carbine booted to his saddle, so that made it impossible for Beau to have perhaps fired at a wolf or a coyote.

It was the horse they saw first, grazing calmly along, reins dragging. They didn't see Beau until they were close enough to excite the horse.

He was lying on his face, one arm curled under him, the other arm out flung. Jase left his saddle on the fly, Red and Mike doing the same. McClure, though, did not drop down beside the sheriff as quickly as the others did. He remained in a half-crouch, carbine in both hands, turning around very slowly probing the settling night. But there was no one to be seen out there, nor heard either.

Jase made the first rough examination and sat back. "Broken collarbone," he said. "We got to tear off his shirt, Mike, and tie off that bleeding. He's leaking like a stuck hog."

Howell was good at this sort of thing. In fact, he was better at it than Jason, so Jase did as Mike said, and they both got covered with Sheriff Beaufort's blood before they had the bleeding halted, at least slowed considerably.

McClure stood by. When the bandaging was almost

finished he said, "Want me to go back and fetch the buckboard, Boss?"

Jase nodded without speaking or ceasing at his work. McClure got back astride, hooked his horse hard back westerly, and rode like a Comanche, with his carbine held aloft in one hand.

Beau was as limp as a rag, and gory-looking even in the darkness, but Mike was fairly confident. "He'll make it. Be a while, but he'll pull through all right." Then, as they finished and looked at one another across the sprawled man, Mike said, "What in tarnation *for*?"

Jase had no idea, but one thing was certain; it hadn't been any accident, and if the light had been better, Beau probably would have been killed outright.

CHAPTER ELEVEN

THERE WAS BOUND TO BE A LOT OF TALK IN TOWN, when the Hurd ranch men brought in Sheriff Beaufort with a bad wound, semi-conscious, and unable to give much of an account of what had happened.

He had been loping along expecting nothing. He hadn't seen a man or a horse, or even a cow. The next thing he remembered was being hoisted into the back of Jase Hurd's buckboard feeling like he was on fire.

Archer Grant's little wizened, pinched face showed anxiety mixed with skepticism as he sidled over to Howard Meredith and said, "Got a mighty bad smell to it, if you ask me, Howard. First, young Hurd brings in a dead outlaw—then he brings in Beau."

Old Evan Forsyth, standing nearby in the crowded small office of the jailhouse while Jase and Beau were out back in one of the cells where Claude Clymer was working over the town marshal, looked stonily at Archer, but he said nothing, and neither did anyone else who heard that remark, until Mike Howell, over by the door re-telling how they had found Beau, very slowly turned and said, "Mister Telegraph man, if you got somethin' to say against Hurd, why don't you just out and say it?"

Young Jim Forsyth frowned at Howell. "Forget it," he growled, as Jase emerged from the back room looking grey and troubled. Young Forsyth said, "How is he, Jase?"

"Well, the preacher says he's a lot better'n he looks, but that was one hell of a wound, and he's got blood all over him."

"You too," someone murmured, and Jase looked down. He had, for a fact, been smeared with a lot of Beaufort's blood.

The liveryman shoved a cup of hot coffee at Jase. "We'll make us up a posse come daylight," said the liveryman, "and if that feller left any tracks at all, believe me, we'll run him down."

There arose a general sound of grim assent as Jase tasted the coffee. It was as bitter as acid, but he was not in the mood for noticing that.

The saloon owner guided Jase through the crowd and to the plank walk beyond. Out there, he said, "You watch where you're riding on the way home tonight, Jase. When a man gets bushwhacked the way Beau did tonight—in the dark, ridin' across another man's land—it could damned well be a case of mistaken identity. It's happened before."

McClure and Howell came clumping out and as Jase turned to go to the wagon with them, he hardly remembered Milner's remark. But a mile out, where they left the road angling westerly and northerly, the warning came back. He dissected it carefully, but, except for the fact that Beau had indeed been on JH range, he was at a loss.

It was Mike Howell who said something that kept Jase thinking of this. Mike was worrying a corner off his plug of chewing tobacco and talking at the same time, which rather garbled the words, but the substance was clear enough.

"One of two things; either Beau stumbled on to someone, or that feller's been skulkin' around, maybe in closer to the ranch, because Beau wasn't more'n a mile out when he got hit . . ." Mike pocketed the plug, pouched his chew, then spoke again. "And we know darned well the sheriff didn't stumble on to no cow thief, or someone like that, because he said himself he didn't see nothin' nor know nothin', until we was lifting him into the wagon. So—that makes it look different from just some wildman ridin' around lookin' for someone to shoot, don't it?"

It did. Jase looked thoughtfully at Mike for a moment. "Why would someone be prowling around the ranch, Mike?"

Howell got a sly, wise look as he answered. "Suppose someone's been on Hickman's trail since he got shot beyond the mountains, Boss?"

McClure butted in. "That don't match, Mike. If someone was trailing him, wouldn't they just maybe ride in lookin' for him? Why would they skulk around, then take a pot-shot at the wrong man?"

"Because," exclaimed Howell irritably, "because they didn't *know* it was the wrong man, Red. They figured it was Hickman."

Jase kept out of this argument. He drifted back to the

76

basic facts, and at least part of what Mike had just suggested worked in very well. Someone *had* been out there, waiting. For Hickman? Maybe, but if that were so, then whoever the bushwhacker was, he hadn't been to town or he'd have heard that Hickman was dead. For Beau? No doubt about it, most lawmen had gun-handy enemies, but if there had ever been one who didn't have, it had to be Jedediah Beaufort. The worst thing he'd ever done was crack some heads in a saloon brawl. Cowboys didn't carry grudges over things like that. Not *killing* grudges.

For Jase Hurd?

What possible reason could there be? Jase had had his share of run-ins over the years, but he'd never shot a man, had never been party to a hanging, hadn't even gone out after rustlers but once, three years back, and that had amounted to nothing at all because they never found the cattle—nor the rustlers.

Jase looked at his riders. "Either one of you got a real hostile enemy? Red?"

McClure shook his head. "Not me, Boss. I steer clear of trouble every chance I got."

"Mike?"

Howell screwed up his face in an effort to manage an honest answer, and spat down the side of the far side front wheel before answering. "Well now, I been riding a lot of years, Boss, and in a lot of different places, and naturally a feller makes a few enemies. But so help me, I can't think of one that'd try to hound me down like this. Mostly, since I don't work the same range more'n a year or two, I'd say that most of the time even my *friends* don't know for sure where I'm at." Howell wagged his head almost dolorously. "I'll tell you something: whoever that bushwhacker is, he's got a *real*

77

grudge."

There was no denying that, but it was no surprise and it did not help Jase rationalize away the shooting of Jedediah Beaufort. By the time they got to the darkened ranch and had put the horses into a rear corral, the moon was almost directly above them, making the yard very bright. McClure paused just inside the barn opening peering around.

"Good night for back-shooting," he said. Then he looked at Jase. "You know what I think?" Red lifted an arm and pointed over in the direction of the canvas-topped wagon. "That's maybe as far as that feller had to sight on a man on a horse. Boss, I could hit a man square through the head at that distance, with the moon this bright."

Mike exploded in disgust. "You danged feather brain, there *wasn't* no moon. It wasn't up yet, when we heard that gunshot. Come along and let's get to bed." Howell went stamping off with McClure following meekly after him.

Another time, Jase might have smiled. Now, he simply leaned on the side of the barn very slowly and methodically trying to fit some facts together in order to create some kind of order. He failed, so he tried again—and again—and he still failed, so eventually, unmindful of the brightness, he ambled over to the main house and got ready to bed down. The only thought that remained uppermost in his mind just before he sank back and closed his eyes, was the one having to do with the tracks that assassin would have to have left behind.

When he awakened a few hours later and rolled over to look out the window, and saw the first faint, cold pallor, he sighed and got out of bed. With all the furor in town, there would surely be a posse of riders out early.

78

He wanted to get over there first, before a lot of store keepers, saloon men, and livery barn-owners trampled the countryside.

He went alone. Howell and McClure were entitled to another forty winks, and moreover this had nothing to do with what he had hired them for.

There was no one around when he reached the place where Beau's blood still dully glistened in the grass, but it was also too dark to read sign, so he dismounted and went very carefully out and round on foot, not really expecting to find much. Nor did he find anything, until the sky turned a quick, greeny shade of wet blue, then he found where a mounted man had stepped to earth, had knelt, and although he found no cartridge casing, he could visualize the ambusher taking aim, and letting Beau right up into his sights.

Maybe a man would remember, after he ejected his casing, to pick it up and pocket it. It did not strike Jase as something the average rider would do. But this man hadn't been an ordinary rider; at least his mission hadn't been the kind of thing an ordinary rider would be involved with.

If a man had *been planning to kill someone*, then he would think ahead to the ejected casing.

Jase loosened the sixgun in his hip holster, got back astride, picked up the tracks and went riding at a slow walk on the assassin's back trail until he was satisfied that the man had, indeed, come from the general direction of his home place. Then he reversed himself and went back to trace out the tracks *after* the shooting. This time the imprints headed almost due north, in the direction of the foothills, or, farther back, the rough, dense reaches of the mountains.

He was a couple of miles out when the sun finally

popped up, like the seed being squeezed out of a grape, and flooded the entire rangeland with warm, golden brilliance. It had been easier to read sign when there was less glare, but, thankfully, the assassin had been traveling fast, this far at least, and a running horse lit down hard and dug in even harder, so the trail was readable all the way to the first gentle rolls of the foothills.

After that, it wasn't so easy to follow; the gunman proved he was no novice by quartering back and forth in search of a creek or some stone outcropping. Jase guessed from this, since there was neither stone nor a creek anywhere close, that the gunman was completely unfamiliar with the countryside. Later, though, where the grassy low hills petered out and the brushy, rougher uplands country began, the gunman found his ledge of stone.

Jase had to leave his horse tied and scout ahead a step at a time to pick up the faintly abrasive scratches horseshoes made over impervious rock. It was very slow and frustrating work. He could look ahead and guess about which canyon the gunman would have to take, if his intention was to try and cross through the cordillera, but if Jase went charging up there—and the gunman swung east or west—Jase would lose him altogether.

Far back someone hooted in a rising shout and Jase looked around. It looked like a platoon of cavalry except that the riders were scattered out left and right. He made a little cairn of stones where he'd stopped in order to be able to find the place again, then turned and went back down where he'd left his horse. The posse men from town arrived where the horse was tied at about the same time.

Howard Meredith, wearing a new hat to shield his pale face, and also wearing a spanking new gun belt, reined up and looked soberly down at Jase as Earl Milner and the others, even including old Archer Grant, came up in a shower of dust. Meredith said, "What did you find, Jase?"

Hurd turned and pointed. "He went up in there, got into some rock, and I quit when I saw you coming." Jase turned back, dropped his arm, and gazed at the eager, bleak faces. "If he went straight on, I reckon a telegram beyond the mountains will take care of that. It'll be some days before he breaks clear on the far side. But if he went east or west . . ." Jase shrugged and reached to untie his horse. "It's going to take a heap of riding, and without meaning any disrespect, I think we'd be better off getting some of the ranchers to lend a few men."

Archer Grant watched Jase mount up through slitted cold eyes. "Mind telling us, Jason, how's come you to be goin' to all this trouble before anyone else could get around this morning?"

Jase closed both hands on top of his saddlehorn and gazed at the wizened, older man. "You really want to know, Mister Grant? Then I'll tell you: because I wanted a look at his tracks before eight or ten fellers from town came charging out here, all flung out, making eight or ten more sets of tracks." Jase looked at the saloon man. "How's Beau this morning?"

Milner answered forthrightly. "Sicker'n a poisoned pup. The preacher's staying with him, though, and there's no one around any better at doctoring." Milner raised his heavy face and considered the mountains. It was obvious what he was thinking: Jase was right, no one whose rear wasn't already calloused from straddling

81

a horse had any business trying to run down that bushwhacker.

CHAPTER TWELVE

BY THE TIME JASE GOT BACK HOME HIS TWO RIDERS were working around the barn and the morning was well advanced. They watched him ride in and were circumspectly quiet until he spoke, so that they could gauge his mood.

He told them where he'd been and McClure leaned on a fork and said, "You should've let me know. I could have tracked him."

Jase considered the cowboy, and decided that before sending Earl Milner and maybe Howard Meredith, the respected merchants from town, to get help from the outlying ranchers, he would return to the mountains with McClure and Howell, and perhaps the three of them could do what had to be done. For a fact, the fewer trackers the more haste, and the less possibility of cluttering up the countryside with tracks.

He knew his riders would be agreeable; cowboys liked their line of work, but they liked even more being able to do something as exciting as man hunting. He mentioned going up into the mountains. Both Howell and McClure brightened at once. Then he said, "I'll tell you something, we don't even know what this bushwhacker looks like. Whether he's young or old, sane, or crazy as a pet 'coon. He could lie up, in there, and pick us off like crows on a fence."

Howell answered that warning in typical fashion. "Maybe there's a reward on him. Imagine pickin' up another five hundred cartwheels."

Jase said, "You haven't picked up the first five hundred yet, and if he gets desperate, or if we crowd him too close, you might never collect any of it."

McClure's black eyes rested for a time upon Jason before the 'breed spoke. "You ain't tryin' to scare us out are you?"

Jase smiled. "That's exactly what I'm trying to do, Red. I need live cowboys, not dead ones."

"Well," retorted the 'breed, "that feller'd have to be a lot better in the woods than I am, Boss, or the boot might fit on to the other foot. I was raised in the mountains."

Mike beamed at McClure. "You tell 'em," he said, and turned towards Jase. "About that reward . . ."

Jase was annoyed. "Would you like to know how the sheriff is this morning?" he asked, looking hard at Mike, and Howell colored slightly.

"Yeah. I was going to ask you that, Boss."

"Sicker'n a pup," stated Jase, and heaved his saddle to the ground. "All right, go catch us three fresh animals, then fetch your carbines and a sock full of grub, and we'll go after Mister Bushwhacker . . . And you can have this lousy reward, too, if there is one."

McClure put aside the pitchfork he'd been leaning upon as though it had suddenly turned very hot, then he and Howell went out back for horses while Jase crossed the yard to the main house for something to eat, and his booted carbine. He also made up a little packet of food, and although the day was warm with a promise of increased heat later on, he took along his jacket.

The pair of range riders were brisk and businesslike, which amused Jase. Since he'd employed them, although both were good workmen, he had never seen such eagerness. There were going to be a couple of very

83

long faces if they caught that bushwhacker and it turned out that he had no reward on his head.

They left the yard on a northerly course with Jase explaining about the tracks he had followed. McClure, for a change, was brusque and taciturn. He kept studying the mountains as they headed up towards them, and when they ultimately reached the spot where Jase had walked back to his tied horse when the townsmen arrived, McClure said, "He ain't going through them mountains," and when both Jase and Mike showed interest McClure pointed to the sign heading northward. "He'd been runnin' that horse for more'n an hour by the time he got up here, and he's a rangeman, so he knew darned well that horse wasn't goin' to be able to pick him up in there very far without a lot of rest." McClure sat a while, hands on top of the saddle horn, considering the lie of land. "No way of tellin' from here, which way he'd turn. One way is as good as the other. We can't waste a lot of time bein' wrong, so I reckon what's got to be done is this." McClure dismounted, handed his reins to Mike, and went ahead on foot following those same marks on the stone Jase had followed earlier. But McClure was much more experienced; where Jase had made slow progress, McClure fairly trotted from stone to stone.

Jase did not mention the little cairn until McClure found it and scratched his head. Then Jase explained, and McClure did not look at the stones again; he skirted around them and began a long, arching curve through the lower tiers of trees, westward. It was such a gradual turning that for a while, in among the trees where it was difficult to keep track of directions, Jase only wondered if they hadn't begun to turn. But McClure knew at once, and where they halted near a dilapidated old rotting log bear trap, McClure removed his hat, mopped sweat from his face with a limp sleeve, and said, "He ain't ridin' fast now." McClure looked off through the distant forest where it was shadowy, even a little menacingly gloomy, and pulled his hat back on again. "He ain't in no hurry at all, now. Boss, you know that country up yonder?"

Jase knew it; he'd been hunting these mountains since he and Frank had first owned rifles. "It keeps curving around the valley for about twenty miles," he told the 'breed. "Plenty of grass and water in the little parks. A man could lie over up in here within a hundred yards of you, and if he was quiet you'd ride right by him."

McClure wasn't worrying about riding *past* the bushwhacker, he was worrying about riding up on to him. An open plain was a lot different; unless a man did as this ambusher had done to Beau—pot-shoot him in the darkness—it was hard to ambush someone in open country. But a forest was made to order for ambushing. *That* was what kept troubling Red McClure, and eventually, another two or three miles ahead, he decided that he did not like the idea of having a pair of mounted men behind him, and, after drinking deeply at a little brawling creek, he said, "Boss, let's you and Mike tie the horses and do the rest of this on feet. A man's a lot smaller target on foot than on horseback, and I got a feeling this bushwhacker might have a camp up ahead not too far."

McClure was right, the bushwhacker did indeed have a camp about three-quarters of a mile onward, but he hadn't been in it since a day or two earlier.

The camp was down close to the edge of the forest. A man sitting secreted up there could look down through the last tree trunk and keep watch over the entire JH range, and he could also see westward towards other

85

outrange.

McClure did his work at the little camp and sauntered down where Mike and Jase were standing, looking down-country, to say, "He went right on by, and he's angling down towards the open country now." McClure held up a hand. "Smokes cigars." He lowered the palmful of chewed butts. "He's got pretty rich taste for a range rider."

Howell said, "Killin' for hire pays better'n riding ranges, Red. Find anything else up there?"

"Yeah. Two things. One's the imprint of what looked at first like a couple of silver dollars placed face down side by side, and the other—"

"Binoculars," stated Jase.

McClure paused briefly. "And the other thing is a lot of boot tracks, and the place where he slept. I can tell you he ain't a very big man. Maybe about Mike's height, and leaner."

They went back, got astride again, and let McClure track the assassin down to where he left the trees and skirted along the edge of the range. McClure would have continued but Jase growled at him. "You know better'n that. He's got binoculars. The only reason he rode out of the trees was so that anyone following his sign would do the same thing—and he's sitting up there somewhere in the shade, watching his backtrail with those damned binoculars."

McClure pondered that, then apparently decided it was right because he hauled back and rode onward again, but without leaving the protection of the forest.

They eventually found where the ambusher cut back into the trees, and a mile farther they came upon the place where he had off-saddled in a grassy little glade beside an ice water creek, and took the rest he had needed since reaching the mountains in a dead run from that place where he'd shot Sheriff Beaufort.

In this place McClure scuttled around like a hunting dog on the trail of a hiding grouse. He found another gnawed cigar butt, and he also found the imprints where a man had sat, cleaning his carbine. The man appeared to have kept facing his backtrail. He had eaten, too. McClure found an empty oyster can and a crumpled scrap of paper from some salted biscuits. There was still salt on the paper, but there wouldn't be for long; if there was one thing small animals cherished above all other things, it was salt, and they'd come for miles to devour a paper, or a man's shirt, or a saddle blanket, or even a bridle, to get salt.

McClure reported his finds and Jase stood gazing out towards the open country trying to understand what the fugitive was doing. Getting away, of course, from the place where he had—or so he probably thought—killed a man. But unless he had some idea about circling the entire vast distance of Carter Valley, he was not doing a very good job of getting clear. If he had remained on a due westerly course instead of following round as the mountains curved, he would by now be several miles along in a direction that was better for him, than making this big half-circle, which did not actually take him very far beyond the line of pursuit.

Even assuming, as seemed plausible, that the fugitive did not know the country very well, he was not blind, and in daylight it was plain enough that by riding on westerly the land became less mountainous, less difficult to cross through, and therefore more amenable to his requirements.

But he wasn't traveling west.

A mile onward McClure crumbled some dirt and said

their man was probably no more than a couple of hours ahead of them. He had wasted quite a bit of time back there, letting his horse rest and fill up.

Jase finally called a halt where the tracks led out of the forest again. "This lad's no greenhorn, but I'll be damned if I can figure out what he's doing." McClure pointed to the range yonder and started to say something but Jase did not allow him much of a chance.

"He cuts in and out of the trees so that anyone trailing him will do the same, and he can see how many there are of them, and how far back they are. That's pretty easy to figure, but what I *don't* understand is why he's not leaving the valley. We're skirting around is all. If we keep at it long enough, unless he breaks off and heads into the mountains somewhere, we're all of us going to end up out front of the rooming house in Junction."

Mike Howell skived a thin sliver off his cut plug and carefully plucked the pocket lint from it before popping the tobacco into his mouth. He leaned upon a big red fir and eyed his companions before saying, "The trouble with trailin' a man is that you don't never really catch up until he stops. I've done this must be fifty times in my life, and about forty of them times all I got out of it was a sightin' over a lot of strange country, and a saddle sore." Mike spat. "The best trackers I ever rode with eventually figured a man out from his sign, then figured on up ahead of him, and when the fugitive come along—there we was, in the trail waiting for him."

McClure seemed to take this as some kind of oblique reflection upon his tracking ability, because his black eyes turned baleful and he said, "Mike, all's I'm doing for you fellers is *find* the man's track. I ain't *makin'* them."

Those two were about to start one of their little bickering arguments and Jase wasn't in the mood for it, so he broke it up with a suggestion. "Suppose you two keep on the tracks, and as soon as I can find a place where I can climb up high enough, I'll try and pick him out as he moves and see where he's headed. Then I'll catch up and maybe we'll do what Mike said—get ahead of him."

McClure and Howell exchanged a look and neither of them showed much enthusiasm. Mike said, "You're the boss. We'll travel slow enough for you to catch up."

They parted at this spot, but it didn't last long. Less than a quarter-mile farther along McClure found a place where the man they had been trailing rode into the camp of two other men, who evidently had been expecting him, or maybe awaiting his arrival, and this changed a lot of things, including the odds, so Mike sent Red to backtrack, find Jase and fetch him to the three-man camp.

Jase hadn't been traveling fast so McClure found him rather quickly, and they went back together to the place where Mike was sitting disconsolately upon a deadfall leg, chewing his cud and waiting.

CHAPTER THIRTEEN

JASE'S REACTION TO THIS LATEST DISCOVERY WAS more bewilderment. If there had been three of them right from the beginning, then why had only one ridden down to JH range to shoot Beau while the other two loafed up here?

The camp, said McClure, was only a day old, and that opened up a possibility that the other two men had only arrived the day before, but that still didn't explain everything to Jase's satisfaction, because after the assassination attempt the bushwhacker had known where to meet his companions.

"Maybe," suggested Mike, "they didn't figure to meet until after the shooting, but I'll tell you one thing: now we know why this bushwhacker didn't keep going west when he should have. He had to meet up with these other two."

Jase was exasperated enough to say he'd give a good horse to understand what was going on, and Red McClure grinned.

Mike Howell, though, was not in very high spirits, for one thing they had been moving a long time, for another Mike didn't like the odds, and after they had retrieved their horses and were mounted again, he said he felt like "One of them moving ducks in a shootin' gallery."

Jase's answer to that, as they took up the fresh trail, shut Mike up. "You don't expect that feller to just fall down on his knees and beg you to take him and collect the reward, do you?"

Howell moped along for perhaps fifty yards, then he brightened. "Hey, there's *three* chances we'll collect reward money now, Red."

McClure, who was not as eager for the money, twisted in the saddle to say, "Yeah, Mike. And there's also three times the chances now, we'll get shot at."

The trail was easier to follow with more than one horse making tracks, but Jase's bafflement deepened as the tracks continued on around through the lower slopes in among the trees, skirting the valley as before. It was beginning to look like his prediction about all of them meeting out front of the boarding house in Junction was going to come true.

Finally, when they halted at a creek to tank up the horses, Jase began to form a vague idea, and it was based upon that premise Earl Milner had first voiced the previous night in town: someone had shot the wrong man; they had been looking for someone in particular, and Beau had resembled him in the darkness, and the *reason* they had shot him was because there weren't *three* of these men, there were *four* of them—and the fourth one had done something the other three wanted his hide for.

Hickman! The only person Jase could imagine who might have done something worth getting himself killed over was Houston Hickman. And that story Hickman had told of being shot while trying to stop a stage was probably a lie; at least it probably was not the entire truth. Perhaps Hickman *had* halted the coach, and had robbed it, and had afterwards tried getting away with all the plunder.

He was jarred from his speculations by Red halting up ahead with his arm raised, staring directly ahead through the gloom and trees. Howell eased out his carbine as he stopped beside Jase.

McClure did not move for a moment, then he lowered his arm, slumped, and twisted to say, "Damned lousy bear. I thought sure we was in an ambush."

Mike shoved the carbine back into its boot with a solid curse, and glared his disgust at McClure's back as they started onward again.

Jase did not go back to his speculations after this; somewhere up ahead were three dangerous men. If they did decide to back track and make certain they were not being followed, a man riding along with his thoughts in the clouds could very easily wind up belly-down across his saddle.

Finally, about twelve miles from where they had first entered the mountains, it became evident to them all that Jase's earlier questions were valid; they were, in actual fact, making a complete circle of the valley. Where they halted to consider this, near a clearing, McClure broke out his little packet of food, and this reminded Jase that he too was hungry, so they dismounted, loosened the cinchas and let their horses graze the clearing while they sat down in tree shade to eat.

"We can keep trailing," said Jase, "and with a lot of luck maybe catch up to them tonight, late. Or we can go back, get fresh horses at the ranch, and cut straight southward across the valley to the mountains down there, which is a hell of a long ride, and try to find their sign over there—providin' they haven't turned off somewhere between here and there."

Mike said, "Where would they turn off? You know this country. What's on across the valley?"

"Nothing, until they reach the south stage road, and that can't be why they're going out and around like this. Hell, if all they'd wanted to do was leave the valley, they could have done it back a half-dozen miles just by keeping to the low country to the west. It's not the road."

McClure had a thought. "You don't reckon they're figuring on robbin' the town, do you?"

Jase did not know about this, and had not considered it. Of course it was a possibility, but it seemed to him that outlaws intent upon robbing a town wouldn't advertise their presence by first shooting someone and rousing the entire community.

Mike said, "Let's go back," and that is what they did. After eating and resting their animals, they turned back.

There was a lot of distance to be covered and it was

already beginning to look like darkness would overtake them before they reached the place where they had entered the mountains earlier, but they were not tired nor hungry—just puzzled and intrigued. Something had happened to dispel Mike Howell's earlier disillusionment, and Jase thought he knew what it was; he did not particularly approve, but if Mike wanted to consider himself a bounty hunter, that was his concern.

When they finally reached the home place it was not only dark, but it had been dark for several hours with no sign of the moon. But there were compensations. For one thing it was a warm night, for a change, and for another thing, when they off-saddled and went to catch fresh horses, it seemed that they might be closing in a little on their prey.

McClure said he wished Sheriff Beaufort were up and around; he thought a little reinforcing along the way might help a lot.

They got some more food, then rode out for the second time, but this time in darkness, and riding southward, and as they passed the main house Mike turned and said, "Boss, you forgot to close the door over there."

Jase looked, not really concerned. There had once been a big lock for the door of his house, but no one had seen it, or remembered what had become of it, in over forty years.

Jase hauled up short, not because the door was open, but because he remembered slamming it closed. He reined around and walked his horse back as far as the porch steps, and sat gazing up there. Then he said, "Damnation," and stepped to earth with Mike and Red watching.

He reached the porch, peered in, saw the devastation,

93

and stood in the doorway for a full minute before turning and beckoning. McClure and Howell came up, then stared. "You been robbed," said Red, sounding as incredulous as he looked. "Who'd want to go and do that?"

Jase did not enter. He turned and went to lean on the porch railing looking down across the yard. Mike and Red looked at one another, puzzled.

Jase almost felt like smiling. So it *had* been Hickman.

He straightened up and jerked his head. "Let's get to riding," he said, and Mike Howell, more bewildered than ever, asked if he hadn't ought to close the door. Jase looked back. "If you want to. They didn't get anything. There's nothing in there they'd want. Hurry along."

As they wheeled away from the house Jase pointed his horse in a new direction, southeastward towards Junction. Finally, he explained.

"I don't know the details, but I'll tell you what I've figured out so far. Hickman came through the mountains, like we figured, and he'd been shot on the far side—not by some stage passenger, but by one of those three men who came down through the mountains behind him. They were scouting up the ranch, maybe all day yesterday, maybe just after dusk last night. That would be possible because those other three only got over to Carter Valley maybe yesterday morning. The other one—he may have pushed on ahead; at any rate he knew Hickman was on the ranch."

"How?" demanded Mike, and for once Red made Howell look bad by saying, "By that liver-chestnut horse, can't you figure that out? We turned him out, didn't we, and how many liver-chestnuts you seen around the country?"

"All right, all right," snapped Howell. "You don't have to keep saying it over and over."

Jase laughed, this time. Then he continued speaking. "When Beau rode for town that feller was out there waiting. He probably thought it was Hickman, or maybe he thought it was me—he figured either Hickman or I knew something, and he didn't want either of us to get to the sheriff in town with it. Only he shot the sheriff."

"Knew what?" demanded Howell.

Jase expelled a big breath. "My brother and Hickman made a six thousand dollar raid down in Denver just before the law caught Frank and hanged him. Maybe it was the six thousand those three were after; maybe it was something don't any of us know about, but if they tried to kill Hickman it was because he knew where the six thousand was cached, or whatever it was, and maybe they figured he'd told me."

"Why would he tell you?" Mike asked.

Jase looked around. "They ransacked the house, didn't they, Mike? Do you figure they did that just for exercise?"

Howell said, "I'll be damned. You might be right. And they wasn't up ahead of us after all, was they?"

Jase nodded. "Yeah, and they're still ahead of us. What they did was keep going on around the valley to sort of mark time, sort of keep moving and be sure there wasn't a posse on their tails, then they cut diagonally across the southerly range and came back here to the ranch, looking for something Hickman—or I—had hidden. Like that six thousand dollars, maybe."

Red McClure was impressed. "Hey, Boss, you'd ought to take over the sheriff's office. You're a pretty good detective."

Mike neither agreed with this nor disagreed with it.

"What's the sense of riding to town, then?" he asked. "I know we can't track them in the dark, but of all the directions they'd head in after raiding the ranch, it wouldn't be towards town, Boss."

"Mike, I think that's exactly where I'd ride if I was in their boots. Hickman's dead. By now they know that. They think I've got whatever Hickman had. They searched the ranch and couldn't find it. So—what they need is me; the man they figure can tell them where it is." Jase pointed off where Junction's lights shone faintly in the empty night. "Since they don't know we rode our tails off trying to track them down today, and since we weren't at the ranch, why then—"

"Yeah, I see," muttered Mike, also staring at those distant lights. "They figure you're in town maybe playin' a little poker or bellying up to the bar."

Jase thought this had to be about it. He did not give much thought to what Hickman's former associates were after. He was satisfied, though, that they were after *something*, and just before reaching town, when Mike let off a little squawk, Jase knew exactly what was coming.

"Hey, Hickman didn't have nothing on him when we searched him in the barn, Boss. Ain't that right?"

Jase said, "Plumb right, Mike."

"Then by gawd he cached it somewhere. Maybe in the barn. Maybe in the corral or out somewhere on the range." Howell bent forward to see McClure on Jase's opposite side. "Red, that couple hunnert reward for Hickman keeps lookin' smaller and smaller all the time. Maybe Hickman had five, six thousand dollars on him, and hid it."

McClure was perfectly at home in hundreds of dollars, but *thousands* of dollars, well, that was just

96

plain preposterous. McClure settled back as the town lights came closer, and replied quietly to Howell.

"You better take the tie-down off your gun, Mike, and start watching a little out, in case them boys is up there in town, and to hell with that money until afterwards."

Jase smiled. Every now and then the 'breed came up with some solid, common sense. As they approached the outskirts of town Jase thought of something else; in a place no larger than junction was, picking out strangers shouldn't be difficult. If there were *three* of them, and they looked tough and camp-stained . . . Jase also reached down and tugged loose the little leather tie-down that fitted over the hammer of his holstered sixgun to keep the weapon from falling out when he rode fast.

CHAPTER FOURTEEN

THEY CAME INTO JUNCTION FROM THE SOUTHWEST because that made the livery barn handy when they dismounted. The nighthawk met them out front with an expression of disgust. As he took their reins he said, "If you fellers figure to get a drink at Milner's place you'd better just buy a bottle and guzzle it outside."

Mike and Red glanced up the road as though they expected some visual reason for that advice to manifest. It didn't, and Jase said, "Are they having a wake up there?"

"Naw," exclaimed the nighthawk. "Southbound coach busted an axle just north of town and they didn't have the stand-by stage ready, so them folks got to spend the night in town. It ain't even Sat'day night, by gawd, and a local man with a right at the bar can't hardly worm his

97

way up there for strangers. And cowboys. One of the outfits southeast o' town took delivery on a herd that was trailed up from Arizona." The hostler turned and went stalking down into the barn, and Mike Howell expressed Jase's thoughts.

"With a townful of strangers, how do we pick out them three—*if* they came here?"

Jase had speculated beyond that. "From being the hunter, I've become the hunted. Those boys'll have the advantage, Mike. Most folks can point me out to them."

McClure, who had been quiet up until now, still stood gazing up the roadway. Junction seemed a little livelier tonight than it usually did, but not too noticeably noisy nor rowdy.

Big Jim Forsyth appeared wearing a coat over his blue shirt. He was also wearing his stiff-brimmed hat on the back of his head, and a freshly oiled pair of boots. Except for the badge on his shirtfront Jase would have thought Jim was on his way to someone's shindig at the south end of town. The badge, and the look on Forsyth's face as he recognized Jase and ambled over, suggested something else.

"Put in a hard day at the forge," he said, by way of greeting, "and now, because there's a herd of strangers in town, look what I become."

McClure grinned, but no one else did. Jim wasn't just feeling sorry for himself, he was truly disgusted.

Jase considered asking about three travel-stained strangers, but in the light of the nighthawk's remarks he let that slide for the time being and asked how Beau was coming along.

Jim Forsyth's answer was in the same disgruntled tone. "All right, I reckon. Leastways he was able to smile when paw and the others brought me over to get this lousy badge." Forsyth's expression changed slightly. "Did you boys go man hunting today?"

Jase nodded. "Yeah. We're still man hunting. The feller who shot Beau had some friends waiting for him. We think they probably came to town early this evening."

Forsyth's eyes widened. "Here, in town?" and before Jase answered Forsyth swore. "Damn it all, I *told* 'em I wasn't a lawman, I'm a blacksmith. We'd better go up and talk to Beau, he's still at the jailhouse."

They trooped up there, all four of them, and Preacher Clymer met them sitting at Beau's desk playing solitaire. He was a gaunt six-footer, with an unruly shock of grey, curly hair. At one time he'd been a soldier, and Jase had never forgot the language he had used the time Earl Milner's fine harness racer kicked him in the shin down at the livery barn. At the time Jase had been about thirteen years old, and although he understood *why* that kind of language had been required, and had been willing to admit to himself that it made Preacher Clymer seem more of a man, it had also made him seem less of a preacher.

As they walked in out of the night Clymer met them with a nod and a comment. "You boys don't want to stay in there with him too long, he needs his rest." Clymer played a card, examined it critically, then said, "He's doing pretty good, all things considered. The doctor from over by Yellowstone'll be along in a day or two. I sent him a telegram this morning and he answered this evening. He's got a couple other calls to make down here." Clymer played another card, and that one did not inspire him either.

Jase led the way into the cell room where a lamp was burning, and his first glimpse of Beau made him wonder

99

why Clymer had claimed Beau was doing well; he looked whiter and sicker than he had looked the previous night, if that was possible. But he surprised Jase. When the four of them crowded inside the cell Beau opened his eyes, looked around, then faintly smiled.

"If you're pallbearers you're sort of early, my nose is still warm."

Jase pulled up a stool, sat, then smiled. "Just thought we'd come in and maybe witness your will," he said, and Beau's smile heightened as he softly called Jason a bad name.

Jim Forsyth loomed large over against the front wall of the cell and Beau looked at him with a cynical expression. "You got the size for the job," he murmured, "but I don't think you got the mean streak to go with it, Jim."

Forsyth agreed. "Don't have the mean streak, Beau, and don't have the hankering either." He patted the low slung holstered Colt. "I'm no good with this thing. They could have found someone better, seems to me."

Beau wasn't very sympathetic. After all, prior to his injury he'd been doing that same thing every night *and* every day. "Just don't draw the gun and you'll be all right," he advised. "Anyway, nothing ever happens around here."

Jason cleared his throat. "Bunch of Arizona cowboys in town tonight, Beau. Had you heard that?"

Beau had heard it. "Somebody told me. But they won't make much trouble—unless of course they get drunk, and I talked to Earl about that a while back. He promised to commence watering down his liquor as soon as any of them get noisy."

"And I figure the man who shot you, along with three

100

of his friends, is in town, too," said Jase.

Beau rolled his head weakly to stare. "That don't make a whole lot of sense, Jase."

For a fact, it didn't. Not until Jase took ten minutes to explain what he and his riders had done since morning, and why they had decided, finally, that not only had Beau been ambushed by mistake, but that now it was Jason's turn, and he was fairly certain the attempt would be made—not to kill him; at least not right off—but at least to capture him. He also explained why he thought those men were going to do this if they could, and Beau sighed, lay back a moment staring at the log ceiling, then he presaged his next statement with a groan and a small curse.

"I checked on that story Hickman told you about being shot trying to stop a stage. Well, it happened all right, about a hundred and fifty miles up-country, but the feller who shot him wasn't a passenger, he was a payroll guard for one of those big copper mines up north, and he didn't shoot Hickman until he'd emptied the payroll box and filled his saddlebags with the cash, and was turning to ride off. The guard didn't have a decent chance to fire until then. The last any of them saw, Hickman was hanging to the horn and his horse was running towards the mountains like a scairt rabbit. They still have posses out, up there, looking for him, only they figured he'd be dead by now."

"Any mention of other men around?" asked Jase.

"Nope. It was claimed to be a one-man job." Beau rolled his head sidewards again. "You sure he rode up and met these other men? It couldn't have been some cowboys, or maybe some grub-liners you were following, could it?"

McClure answered that. "There was only one set of

101

ought-size horseshoes, Sheriff, leading away from where you was shot. We followed them same tracks all the way. It was him all right—whoever he is—and them other boys was up there waiting for him, but I figure from the sign them other boys didn't get over and set up camp until yesterday."

Jim Forsyth, who had been listening closely, rolled his eyes and turned with a dolorous expression to Mike Howell. "How'd you like to be deputized into an assistant town marshal for tonight?" he asked, and Mike looked shocked.

"Me, a lawman? No thanks, Mister Blacksmith. I'd as leave be a . . ." Mike, considering Forsyth's size and heft, swallowed, groped for something other than what he had almost said, which was 'dogcatcher'. "I'd as leave be a preacher."

Clymer appeared behind them in the little corridor and gave Mike a long look, but then he ignored them all but Jase. "Visiting time is up, Jason. We all want Beau to get well soon, don't we?"

Jase stood up. He and Beau exchanged a wink, then Jase led the way back out to the front office, and Preacher Clymer closed the door behind himself as he smiled coldly at Mike.

"There are a heap worse things to be than a preacher, cowboy, and if you was to up and ask me, I could name *one* of them right easy."

Jase headed off an argument by opening the front door and jerking his head for Mike and Red to precede him outside. Jim Forsyth followed along, the last one through the door.

Someone up at Milner's saloon was playing a banjo to the accompaniment of a mouth harp. The place was a blaze of light. Otherwise, Junction was quiet and more or less dark, but there were a number of small groups of men standing here and there, mostly in the vicinity of the saloon, talking and smoking. It was a pleasant, clear, warm night. Not everyone wanted to drink, evidently.

Howell said, "Pick any three, Boss," and this was a prophetic innuendo; most of those men up there were range riders, they all dressed pretty much alike, and they had all been living in cow camps for a long while, since leaving Arizona with the beef herd, in fact, so they looked the same as the men Jase wanted to locate would also look.

Jase had a hunch. "You boys go on up and have a drink. I'll be along later." He turned and went hiking back down towards the livery barn. Mike and Red gazed after him for a moment, then turned obediently towards Milner's place. Only Jim Forsyth was left in limbo, and Jim decided to go with McClure and Howell, so he turned in the opposite direction from which Jason was striding.

What Jase had in mind was fairly simple. Cowboys, unless they expected to spend a night in town, usually did not spend the money to stable their horses, they left them tied at the racks along Main Street. But it was possible that other men, who *might* be expecting to be in town a little longer, might leave their stock at the livery barn.

It was just an off chance, but unless he wanted to be someone's sitting duck, he had to find *them* before they found *him.*

The nighthawk was in the harness room taking a long pull from a small bottle and evidently had not heard Jase coming, because when Jase opened the door and poked his head in, the hostler almost strangled on a big swallow. Afterwards, he coughed, his eyes watered, and as he slapped the cork back into the bottle he said, "Lord a'mighty, mister, you scairt hell out'n me. I thought it was the boss. He's dead against a feller drinking a little on the job."

Jase, who knew the liveryman, did not comment. He'd seen the nighthawk's boss so drunk he couldn't find the ground with both hands. But not at the barn. Very few stockmen, whether liverymen or cowmen, tolerated drinking around barns of livestock. "I'm looking for three horses some feller may have left here about an hour after sundown," he said. "They'd be pretty well ridden down because they've been on the trail a lot lately."

The hostler scrabbled under a pile of mouse-gnawed feed sacks to secrete his bottle before straightening around to be helpful. "Well, some of them Arizonans left horses with me this evening, mister. Maybe five or six of them. The others got their horses tied up through town. Would you recognize these horses, maybe?"

Jase not only wouldn't recognize them, he began to see that his hunch was petering out. "These men weren't Arizonans," he said, and stepped back as the hostler came out of the harness room. "Just three riders from up north."

The hostler scowled in concentration, then waved an extended arm. "See for yourself, if you'd like. There's a horse in every stall, and out back we got some in the corrals. It's a little cheaper, back there." The hostler suddenly brightened. "Maybe you'd know the saddles. I could show you—"

Jase said, "No thanks," and turned to somewhat aimlessly walk down the barn looking in the stalls. Most of the horses had been cuffed, so they didn't show much travel stain, and they were all lean and hard-muscled

104

from use. He covered both sides of the barn without knowing what to look for, and without getting any fresh thoughts, then he went to stand in the dark rear doorway gazing out towards the corrals where there were more horses, trying to figure out another way to identify the ambusher and his friends.

The hostler, perhaps being so helpful because of the liquor-guzzling interlude, ambled back there and pointed. "One of them horses is a mighty nice animal. The others look pretty much mustang. It's that liver-chestnut yonder, behind the big bay mare."

Jase straightened up very slowly, looking out where the hostler was pointing. It was too dark to see well, so he walked out there.

CHAPTER FIFTEEN

HE RECOGNIZED THE LIVER-CHESTNUT BEFORE HE'D even climbed over into the corral to get closer. The hostler remained outside, leaning and watching. "Don't get very many like that one," he drawled towards Jason's back. "There's some mighty fine breeding in his background somewhere, wouldn't you say?"

Jase answered quietly as he ran a hand up under the gelding's mane and felt for the brand. "He's got quality to him all right." The brand was there. He moved the hair aside and saw it, then he patted the horse, scratched his withers, which the gelding appreciated, and turned back. "Who owns him?" he asked, as he came to the poles and straddled the top one to drop down outside.

The hostler, still leaning comfortably and looking in, answered casually. "I don't know who he is, mister. Sort of wiry, tough-looking feller. Rode in maybe an hour before you fellers come along."

Jase regarded the hostler. "Alone?"

"Yeah, he come in alone. Asked where the café was, give me a half-dollar, and walked off. I ain't seen him since." The hostler straightened up, turned, then said, "Want to see his outfit?"

Jase nodded and they went back up to the harness room. Saddles hung from wall pegs by one stirrup on all four walls. Harness was racked up on three-tiered sawhorses. The saddle the hostler lay a hand upon was worn and nondescript. So was the bridle that had been draped from the horn. The blanket was fairly new, but it told Jase nothing. There was a blanket roll behind the saddle, and a pair of small bags were tied over the rear skirts, but as much as Jase would have liked to look into those bags, and to unroll those blankets, he couldn't very well do it with the nighthawk standing there, so he went back out into the poorly lighted runway, and when the hostler came out he said, "I think that's one of the men I'm looking for."

The hostler nodded. "Well, if it's to set him to work, mister, maybe you'd do better to just go on back to the ranch and wait for him to come out, because from the looks of him I'd say he's been dry a long while. Tonight he'll be swabbing out his gullet."

Jase smiled perfunctorily. "Yeah, maybe. Did a couple of other fellers, strangers, come along maybe a little later, who looked like they'd been on the trail too?"

The hostler threw up his hands. "Mister, this has been one of the worst nights since I been working here. Riders been coming in by the ones and twos and threes since suppertime. You know, a nighthawk usually don't have to work too hard. That's why some of us fellers'd rather work nights than days. Yeah, there's been at least six, seven, double sets ride in since that wiry cowboy come along, and they all looked like they'd been on the trail."

Jase dug around, found a silver half dollar, and handed it to the hostler, who regarded it with surprise. "What's this for?" he asked. "Hell, we was just killin' time."

Jase said, "Keep it anyway," and started to turn away when something in his memory made him pause. He turned back. "Mind if I have another look at that saddle?" he asked, and the hostler threw apart his arms.

"Look at anything you want around here, mister. Just help yourself."

Jase returned to the harness room, studied the saddle where it hung, then lifted it down and balanced it upon his hip. What he'd observed before without really heeding it at the moment, was that while the saddle had been hanging up there, the left side stirrup had been dragging the floor but the other stirrup, the one hooked over the wooden peg, had looked shorter.

It was. When the saddle was balanced evenly, the right side stirrup leather was at least three inches shorter than the left stirrup leather. Jase hung the saddle back upon its peg, then lifted the seating leather on the right side to examine the crease in the stirrup leather to see if it had been changed recently. It hadn't, and that had to mean that the man who had been riding this saddle had a right leg shorter than his left leg, otherwise— especially if he had come through the mountains on Hickman's trail, which was hard riding—he'd certainly have adjusted his stirrups so that they were both equal.

Jase went back outside and up to the empty doorway. The hostler was nowhere in sight. If Jase had wanted to do a little speculating he could have come up with an idea about this, but he didn't care in the slightest if the nighthawk had *ten* hidden bottles. What he cared about now was finding a lithe, hard-faced, weathered man with a right leg two or three inches shorter than his left leg.

He strolled up the west side of the roadway, hesitated out front of the jailhouse, then decided against worrying Beau, and kept on going until he was opposite Milner's saloon.

Those two musicians who had been playing earlier were silent now, probably getting re-energized at the bar. Jase saw Jim Forsyth talking to some cowboys, and when Jim happened to glance over into the shadows upon the far side of the road and saw Jase, he broke off his conversation and came hustling over. As he stepped up from the roadway he said, "Archer said to tell you he had a telegram for you. I offered to look you up and hand it over, but you know old Archer; he always acts like his telegrams are special dispensations from gawd."

Jase could guess the origin of that message. He thanked Forsyth and went on a diagonal course towards the telegraph office. Old Archer was sitting in there with his eyeglasses on, wearing a green eye-shade too, reading a magazine, and when Jase entered, he leaned to search through some yellow papers in a little box and sift one out.

"From Tabitha Meredith," Archer said, standing to hand the telegram over. "It says she got up there all right, and seen the kid and his maw, but that his two uncles ain't around."

Jase stared at Archer, until the old man sank back down at his desk and became busy there, then Jase read the message. It was essentially as Archer had said. What

108

hit Jase squarely between the eyes as he stood there was that one sentence about Frank's boy's two uncles being gone.

So *that* was who they were. They and Houston Hickman had gone out to rob that payroll stage. The other man would probably be some friend or partner. He pocketed the telegram and got to the door before a fresh idea arrived, then he turned back, picked a slip of paper and a pencil off Archer's desk, and wrote a short message. Archer took the paper and read it aloud for verification. "Does one of them have a leg shorter than his other leg?" Archer pursed his lips, re-read, then reached up to scratch his head as Jase tossed down a crumpled greenback and walked out without speaking.

This time he went all the way back down to the jailhouse. Preacher Clymer wasn't there, fortunately, but the lamps were still lighted. Jase went down to the cell where Beau was lying, pulled up the little stool again, and under Beau's quizzical look, he explained about the saddle with one stirrup shorter than the other one, and about the message from Tassie.

"You sent her a message?" Beau asked.

"Yeah, just now. It gave old Archer fits trying to figure out *what* has one leg shorter than the other leg."

Beau smiled. "Sort of like those conundrums we used to play at when we were kids. Well, how can you be so sure this hop-legged feller is one of them?"

Jase had forgotten to explain about the liver-chestnut. He did that now, and Beau thought a while before commenting. "They must have found that animal out with your remuda. He must be quite a horse for an outlaw to take the time to rope him on the range and switch saddles."

There was no doubt about that, he *was* quite a horse.

109

And Jase thought it proved a connection between Houston Hickman and the other nightriders, unless they knew that horse, knew how good he was, they wouldn't have stopped to catch him on their ride towards the JH ranch from the westerly range.

Beau, who did not know the horse, was willing to accept this as a possibility, but as he said, they were stringing a lot of beads on an awful weak strand of thread. "Find the hop-legged feller and bring him in," he told Jase. "Tell Jim I said to lend a hand. And Jase—if there is three of them, try and catch the hop-legged one alone, away from anyone. With a town full of strangers, one gunshot could get a lot of folks all stirred up. Especially those Arizona range riders."

Jase stood up, nodding. He hadn't figured on busting into Milner's saloon with a gun in each hand. "Get some sleep," he said from the cell doorway, and the look he got made him laugh as he went back out front.

Preacher Clymer was coming across the road just as Jase stepped out. They met on the plank walk in the darkness under the wooden awning. Clymer looked disapprovingly stern.

"Did you wake him up, Jason?"

"He wasn't asleep, Preacher, but even if he had been, this was no social call," Jase replied, "and I figure on coming back in a little while with someone to be locked up, so if you're going home for the night don't bar the front door."

Clymer stood thoughtfully quiet for a moment. "Serious trouble?" he eventually queried.

Jase started off as he answered. "Maybe. It could be the man who shot Beau."

Clymer stood staring as Jase crossed to the far walk and turned northward up in the direction of the saloon.

110

Then Clymer did the same thing, he also crossed the road, but instead of heading for the saloon, he went down between two store buildings towards the residential section of town; down where Howard Meredith, old Evan Forsyth, and the other town elders lived.

Jason shouldered his way through a small crowd of cowboys out front of the saloon and entered. The lamplight hit him in the eyes, hard, so he stepped along the wall for a moment, then looked around for Howell and McClure. They were sitting at a table back near the cold big old cast iron stove, and Jim Forsyth was sitting with them, nursing a five-cent beer. Mike and Red each had a half-full shot glass of whisky in front of them.

The room was full, noisy, and smoky. There were a few townsmen on hand, but by and large the customers were range men. Some called a greeting as Jase made his way to the far table. He answered with a wave and kept on easing along until he got to the empty chair and sat down. Jim Forsyth said, "Busy in here tonight as a cat in a box of shavings. Earl's helping out behind the bar, so you *know* it's busy."

That was true; Milner usually tried to keep normal hours and hire night men to run his bar after eight or nine at night. He was past the age when a lot of yelling, exuberant young range hands did anything for him.

Jase explained about the liver-chestnut horse, the saddle with one short stirrup, and the telegram from Tassie Meredith in Cheyenne. Mike and Red hung on every word. So did Jim Forsyth, but he still looked a little self-conscious about wearing that gun and badge.

Howell's Adams apple bobbed up and down as he twisted to scan the boots around their table. "Right or left leg, Jase?"

111

"Right one, Mike. Maybe three inches shorter than his left one."

"Built-up heel," murmured Forsyth, then scowled. "Short of going around through here liftin' up right legs, it won't be easy to find this feller at night, Jase."

Red said, "Does he limp, maybe?"

Jim scowled. "Not with a built-up boot heel."

Earl came along with a flour sack apron tucked into his waistband, looking tired and harassed. When he recognized Jase he leaned down and said, "Know anyone who wants to buy a flourishin' business?"

Jase smiled. "Why sell it? You're getting rich tonight."

Earl's sour expression did not alter. "Yeah? Well, tell that to my feet. I got numb up to the knees couple hours back. Well, what'll you have, Jase, likker or beer?"

Jase said, "Beer," and watched Milner thread his ponderous way through smoke and men and noise back to the bar. He could not remember ever seeing the saloon as crowded as it was this night. He had been there when it had been just as noisy, but never this crowded.

Howell, who was now sitting back in his chair, hat-brim tilted down, making a study of as many of the booted feet as he could see, finally said, "You brought us quite a job, Boss. Maybe what we'd ought to do is split up and go off in four directions, lookin' for this feller."

Howell was probably right, but Jase was beginning to get a feeling up between his shoulder blades; no doubt the man with the shortened leg, and his partners, were looking for Jase about now, just as hard as he was looking for them.

112

CHAPTER SIXTEEN

THERE WAS A POSSIBILITY THAT THE TWO MEN WITH the bushwhacker had not come into town with him. This idea occurred to Jase as he sat sipping his beer and watching the crowded room for sign of a man who might have a slight hitch in his get-along. They hadn't shown themselves last night, during the bushwhacking attempt, and they'd stayed in their distant camp waiting for the bushwhacker to come to them.

The best reason Jase could imagine for men like that to want to avoid being seen, especially in a town, was elemental: they were wanted men, professional outlaws.

So was the bushwhacker, probably, if he was one of the Hickman brothers, but he seemed more strongly motivated. At least that was how Jase worked this all out in his mind. Perhaps the bushwhacker was the leader of the pack. Possibly he had more of a stake in that payroll than the others.

Jase tried to recall whether Beau had said how much money was taken off the coach, and failed. Not that it mattered.

Someone else was also thinking of money. Mike Howell abruptly leaned upon the table and, looking directly at Jason, said, "Did the sheriff know anything in particular about these fellers we're lookin' for?"

Jase regarded Howell a moment, then, with a perfectly straight face, he answered. "That they have two eyes, two legs, two arms, more than likely."

Mike reddened. "Naturally they got them things." He was slightly angered.

Jase relented. "He didn't say anything about the

reward, Mike, but I've been sitting here thinking about something: if they didn't ride into town with the other feller, then they must be a little gun shy about their faces—and that would make a feller with an evil mind like mine think their faces must be on wanted flyers—and *that* means reward money, doesn't it? By the way, what are you and Red going to do with all this bounty money, buy a ranch?" Jase did not give Mike time to answer. He got up from the table and, leaning down, said, "All right, we'll go four different ways. Be careful; if this is the man who tried to kill Beau, you corner him a little and he'll try to kill you also."

The smoke was thicker in Milner's saloon, and the noise had scarcely abated even though it looked to Jase as though the place was not quite as full as it had been a little earlier. Outside, the little lounging groups of talkers were still there. The only genuine drunk was a gangling cowboy that four other cowboys were forcing down over the public water trough across the way. Every time he tried to fight clear or bawl a string of curses, those four "friends' of his would lean, hard, and shove his head under water again. It was a hard way to sober a man up, but in a town full of yeasty men wearing guns, and with their spurs down a notch like a herd of fighting roosters, it might at least keep the drunk cowboy from getting himself killed.

Jase ambled over, not really to watch so much as to assess the right boot and the right leg of each man busy at the trough. There was not a built-up heel there. Nor was there a man with a gimpy way of moving.

Unexpectedly, down at the juncture of the intervening eastward street and the main roadway, five men in dark attire appeared, bunched up and fully armed. No one paid much attention, but Jase did, because he understood the meaning of that little vigilante crowd. He swore to himself and headed down there.

Preacher Clymer was standing with Evan Forsyth and Howard Meredith when Jason walked up to them. Jase shook his head. "Go on back to bed."

Jim Forsyth's father was a tough old character, ham-handed, scarred, as craggy as moss-agate. He was not a tall man, but he had as much solid-packed-down weight and gristle as any man half a head taller. He looked Jase squarely in the eye and said, "Who you think you're talking to, Jason Hurd? When us fellers need a young whippersnapper to tell us what to do—we'll turn over a rock and ask one!"

Howard Meredith was the conciliatory type, but tonight he was also worried and anxious. "Preacher said the man who shot Beau might be in town, Jason. We want him." Meredith raised both hands to clasp the lapels of his coat. He was wearing that new shellbelt again. It had been run out to the last notch to fit round his paunch. He might have *thought* he looked pretty rugged and ominous, but he really didn't. Not to Jase, and not to any of those range riders up the road out front of Milner's saloon.

"Jim is looking for him, so am I, and so are two pretty good men who work for me, Mister Meredith, and if you boys start looking too, it's going to get kind of crowded out here. If you want to do something, just go on down to the jailhouse and be on hand if we find him and fetch him down there." Jase smiled at old unsmiling Evan Forsyth. "I didn't mean any offense," he said. Old Forsyth's stony expression did not change.

One of the men farther back, behind Meredith, said, "Who is this feller, Jase? What does he look like and what's his name?"

115

Jase was beginning to feel exasperated and irritable. "I don't know his name."

"Then how do you know who you're looking for?"

Jase got a good grip on himself before replying. "I don't exactly, except that he's got a little limp, maybe, and is sort of wiry and hard-looking."

Howard Meredith started. "*Him!* Why, hell, that feller was in the store two minutes before quitting time tonight, Jason. He bought a sack full of grub—you know, rider's findings; tinned tomatoes, sardines, crackers, tobacco, some tinned pork and a couple of—"

Jase interrupted. "Whao! Just tell me if he bought enough for three men, for maybe three or four days."

Meredith's frown came down. "I'd figure so, yes. I can tell you it was far too much for one man to eat in a week."

"And when he left the store, did you happen to see where he went?"

Meredith's scowl lingered. "Well, not exactly, except that he cut down towards the livery barn."

Jase stood a long moment staring at Tassie's father. If the bushwhacker had gone down to the livery barn with his sack of provisions—but hadn't ridden out to hand them over to his partners, because if he had the nighthawk would have remembered, and would have mentioned it—why then, the other men *had* come at least to the edge of town, had been given the supplies, and had probably then ridden off. Jase suddenly smiled at Howard Meredith. "Thanks. That helped. Now, would you fellers just go down to the jailhouse and wait—please?"

Evan Forsyth nudged Clymer, who nudged Meredith, and they all trooped on down across the road towards Beau's place, with Preacher Clymer hiking along in the

116

rear. No cow town had ever seen a more unlikely bunch of vigilantes, but if they looked a little incongruous, they wouldn't look the least bit that way hauling on someone's hangrope, and they prepared to do exactly that.

Jase went back up towards the saloon searching for Jim, Mike, and Red. He found his riders easily enough. They were standing together over against the front wall of the harness works, quietly discussing their inability to find anyone with a shortened leg. When Jase came up they told him, in dolorous voices, that they didn't believe the ambusher was still in town. Just to make certain, Jase sent McClure down to the corral out back of the livery barn to look for the liver-chestnut horse, then he sent Mike hunting for Jim Forsyth, and while these things were in process, he did a lot of recapitulating.

If there was only one man in town searching for him, then the advantage had shifted back to Jase again. He at least had others to rely upon. That did not mean he wouldn't have to be just as careful, but it *did* mean once the others were with him, that bushwhacker was going to find his job *four* times as difficult as it had been before.

Jim and Mike came up first. Red McClure was another few minutes arriving to report that the liver-chestnut was still down there, and from the looks of him he hadn't been ridden, let alone saddled, since he'd been turned into the corral.

Jase had two options, as he saw it, and as he explained to the others. They could go, four strong, making a legal, physical search, using Forsyth's badge to make it proper, or Jase could go across the road and take a seat in Milner's saloon right up front, and wait.

Sooner or later the bushwhacker was going to find out who he was, what he looked like, and locate him.

There was not a single dissenting judgment when Jim said, "Go over to the saloon, Jase, and we'll drift in later." Forsyth turned, but both the range men were already nodding agreement.

Jase was perfectly willing. "One of you hang back by the door, and the other two stay on my right and left. If we can take this orang-outang alive, that's what we want." He paused, looking round. "You know, if I've sized this up wrong, and those other two *are* around, the top's going to explode off Earl's saloon when we throw down on the one who comes hunting me."

Forsyth, the reluctant lawman, said, "Let it. You dive for the sawdust and leave the rest to us."

That sounded brave enough, but Jase strode away without being overwhelmed with feelings of inviolable security. More than one man diving under a table had been known to eat off a mantel for a couple of months after bullets flew in a saloon fight.

Two Arizonans were leaving as Jase stepped up to the saloon doors, they held one door for him and he nodded back. Inside, the smoke, if possible, was thicker, but it was no longer as agitated as it had been before; now, it hung about shoulder high, swaying like something ghostly when someone walked past. Over at the bar, where Jase went for another beer, George Milner leaned down, rolled up his eyes and said, "Real cheap. I'll sell real cheap tonight. Just thirty per cent of the net paid to me the first of every month. I'm plumb serious, Jase."

The beer was warmer than usual, which meant that George was dipping lower into the crocks behind the bar. But it was wet and tangy, and that was about all beer had to be; if a man wanted to chill his insides or

118

cool off, he could do it better standing under a water pipe out back of the livery barn, which was where most saddle tramps sluiced off in summertime.

Jase turned slowly and looked around the room. Fully two-thirds of the men who were drinking, talking, or playing cards were strangers to him. He had a little difficulty making out the farthest faces because of the smoke, but he did not see anyone he felt might be the wiry, hard-faced man the hostler had described, so he took his beer to a table and got comfortable, but only very briefly. Old Archer Grant came in, sidled up and got a ten-cent big stein of beer, leveled off the suds with a forefinger, left them on top of the bar, to Milner's disgust, then came over to Jase's table and sat down without being asked.

"Been one hell of a long day," he said. "You know, they got rules now, back east, amongst the telegrapher's brotherhood. A feller don't have to work but eight or nine hours a day."

Jase looked over. "The telegrapher's what?"

Archer drank deeply, sleeved off his lips and said, "Telegrapher's *brotherhood*. You gettin' deef, Jase, at your age? It's sort of like them guilds you read about in the newspapers that they got among them highly skilled artisans in Yurp. You know, places like Germany and France, and—well—over there, anyway." Archer hoisted the big glass and drank deeply again.

Jase eyed the older man without much enthusiasm. He remembered Archer's cold stare when they'd met the day before up where the town posse had ridden to intercept Jason when he'd been tracking Beau's bushwhacker. He thought he knew about what Grant had been thinking then—Jason Hurd was Frank Hurd's brother; if there were outlaws around, it wasn't too odd

119

that they'd turn up where the Hurds lived.

Well, perhaps it was justified. Anyway, you couldn't larrup a man for what he thought, especially a nosy old one like Archer Grant.

Jase sipped, looked around, and left any talking that was to be done to old Archer, but the telegrapher hadn't come to Milner's saloon to talk. He put away that entire quart of beer and rose to depart, hitched up his little pointed shoulders, took careful aim for the door, and moved ahead with the exaggerated dignity of someone who had just overshot their known beer quotient by about a pint.

CHAPTER SEVENTEEN

WHEN IT HAPPENED JIM FORSYTH PROBABLY COULD have eliminated about two-thirds of what ensued by simply reaching out with a mighty hand, but while Jim was an excellent blacksmith who could shoe a deformed hoof or shrink a tire on to a warped wheel, or even create rather elegant scrollwork out of steel and iron for upstairs balconies, as he had admitted himself, and as Jedediah Beaufort had said at least once to Jim's face, he was not as good a law officer as he was a horseshoer.

When the stranger walked in and turned to ask Charley Leavitt, who was standing beside the door on the side opposite from Forsyth, if he'd seen Jason Hurd enter the saloon, Forsyth wasn't watching.

An awful lot of men had entered and departed and Jim was getting a little phlegmatic in the hot and smoky atmosphere. As he had said, when a man put in eight or ten hours in a blacksmith shop, he wasn't likely to be very alert. Jim did not even see the stranger, nor hear him, but he heard Charley Leavitt, who had a deep, resonant voice, when Charley pointed with his pipe stem out where Jase was sitting, and by then Forsyth was too late, the lean, whipcord stranger was already working his way forward among the tables.

Jim looked left and right, saw McClure and Howell, saw them both watching the table as the stranger approached, and Jim reached down to loosen the gun he wore in its holster. He was not a gunman but he was perfectly willing to use his weapon. Like every man in that room, Jim Forsyth held that guns were as necessary as any other frontier tool or implement, but, like the others, he only wore one occasionally, for protection if he felt he might need it, and while he was not the least bit afraid of using it, he was certainly not skilled in its use, only passably capable.

The man who walked up to Jase Hurd and who looked like a slightly worn and hard-used range rider, also looked perfectly able to do anything demanded of him, and probably do it a little bit better than any other cowboy. He had that top hand look.

He was of average height, lean, tanned dark brown, did not carry an ounce of spare meat, and had a bold, hawkish face that was narrow with gunmetal eyes. His expression was not *un*friendly, but he did not look to be a man who smiled often.

Jase knew who he was the instant the man paused and looked down, even before he spoke or leaned upon the table. He did not look *entirely* like the other Hickman, but there was enough resemblance. For as long as they gazed at one another, a matter of seconds, each of them took a swift gauge of the other, then the stranger's long, bloodless lips split outward in a down turning smile and he leaned.

"You Jase Hurd, by any chance?"

Jason, with his right hand lying on top of the table half curled round the beer glass, answered casually. "Yeah. Sit down and have a beer."

The stranger sat, only his left hand showing, and when Jase wig-wagged to George Milner for two beers, the stranger looked around. Over at the doorway Jim Forsyth saw the man's head come up and swing, so Jim casually turned so that the badge did not show.

Milner did not bring the beers, his youthful night man did, and as Jase dropped an extra coin in the plump hand of the barman the lean-faced man picked up one of the glasses and said, "Thanks," before drinking the glass half-empty. As he put the glass down and saw Jase watching him, he said, "I'll tell you how it is, Mister Hurd, I been on the trail quite a spell."

Jase acted as though he understood, and tasted the beer, curious about this man's right boot. He had not seen him moving among the tables so he'd been unable to watch him walk. But he was satisfied about the man's identity.

"Looking for work?" he asked, and the stranger regarded Jase thoughtfully without appearing to relax in his chair.

"Sort of, Mister Hurd, but first off I'd like to show you a couple of horses I got corralled out back of the livery barn that I'd like to sell—cheap. Very good horses, but I don't need 'em no more, and I *do* need a little cash. How about walkin' down there and looking at them?"

Jase saw Howell and Forsyth converging behind the stranger, and he presumed Red McClure was coming up from behind his own chair as well. He acted almost too calm as he said, "Who told you I might be interested?"

The stranger's down-drooping faint smile came up again. "Several fellers around town."

Jase saw Howell and Jim Forsyth reach to draw, and said, "I'll tell you what I'll do, Mister Hickman, I'll keep you from being killed if you'll put that other hand on top of the table, too."

The stranger seemed scarcely to breathe as he stared at Jase. Then, imperceptibly, his shoulders gathered and his body coiled, but it was much too late. Jim Forsyth placed his pistol barrel very gently beneath the stranger's ear, and on the opposite side, Mike Hammer leaned, caught the stranger's wrist in a vice-like hold, and with his other hand, Mike disarmed the lean man.

Very gradually at the nearest tables men nudged one another and jutted chins towards Jase's table. Big Jim Forsyth was visible all over the room, but no one expected to see him holding a gun against someone's head, so it took a little time for that condition to be murmured around. Finally, beyond the bar, George Milner heard the whisper and looked over. No one was moving very much now, but George reached under his bar and came up with a shotgun. He pushed it between two men, growling for them to give way a little, which they did quickly, then George leaned there, his big-bored old double-barreled scattergun looking slightly downward at Jase's table companion.

All the noise that had been so noticeable a moment or two earlier died down so quickly that when George shoved his riot gun over the wooden bartop, that bumpy, abrasive small sound carried over the entire big room.

Jase, holding the stranger's stare, said, "Search him, Jim. He's sure as hell got another weapon somewhere."

Forsyth was rough at it, partly because he was inexperienced, partly because he was much more accustomed to handling horses, mules, and oxen. He found a little pepperbox Derringer and a boot knife, which he tossed on top of the table for everyone to see. In the Southwest, where the Spanish and Mexican influence was strong, boot-knives were no rarity, and people did not take umbrage over a man carrying one, but in the Northwest it was different. Men at the nearest tables gazed from that wicked-bladed knife with bleakly antagonistic expressions. Knives, in their opinions, were underhanded, back-stabbing weapons. It was doubtful from the moment that Forsyth tossed down that knife for everyone to see, that even if he'd handed the stranger back his gun, the roomful of stockmen would have allowed him to walk out without being challenged a dozen times before he reached the door.

And the stranger knew it. He could sense it and he could see it. As Jim Forsyth stepped back, holstering his gun, the stranger twisted to look backwards and upwards. Mike Howell cocked his Colt. That little frightening sound traveled the length and breadth of the room, too. The stranger faced Jase and let his body turn loose. He was in an absolutely hopeless situation, and recognized it.

"How'd you do it?" he asked.

Jase felt no real, deep down antipathy for this man, even though he was sure this was Beau's bushwhacker. "For one thing, by finding the liver-chestnut army horse down in the corral out back of the livery bam. For another thing, we tracked you boys, and when you didn't try to leave Carter Valley when you should have, it had to mean you had more business here. And finally, because someone up in Cheyenne telegraphed me down here that *all* the Hickmans were gone."

The stranger sneered. "Why not just tell the truth,

Hurd? You and Houston settled up and when he died you got his saddlebags and hid 'em."

Jase knew this man's type; all the reasoning in the world would not materially alter his preconceived opinions. "Stand up," he ordered, and shoved back his own chair to also rise.

The stranger obeyed, and at once Red McClure, standing slightly to one side, said, "Look, Mike, built-up heel on the right boot."

The stranger glared at McClure. From over at the bar a leathery older man with a piping voice said, "Hurd, is that Beau's bushwhacker?" And at once Jase could feel the wall of hostility thicken on all sides as this idea closed down upon men's minds. Jase did not answer, he jerked his head doorward. "Hike out, slowly, mister, and don't get foolish because the only friends you've got right now are behind you."

That was the truth. The stranger turned and made his way past seated men, around tables and scattered chairs to the door. As he passed through, someone farther back sang out.

"Get a rope, boys!"

In the starry night Jase waited to be sure his three companions were heading diagonally down towards the jailhouse, then he turned back and stood in Milner's doorway. "Leave it up to the law," he called out. "There's no proof yet. Don't do something you'll be sorry about afterwards." He waited a moment, saw their closed, grim faces, knew he had failed, and stepped back to hurry along after the others.

Only three of those dark-attired vigilantes were still down at the jailhouse. Meredith, Forsyth, and the preacher, but when Jase walked in and saw how they were regarding the prisoner, he wondered if he hadn't wasted his breath back at the saloon. The older men looked just as uncompromisingly deadly as the cowboys up at Milner's place.

Forsyth had the prisoner empty his pockets into his hat, and Jase could see that, finally, the stranger's challenging, dark expression was beginning to show a little genuine fear. The elder Forsyth came forward, pawed through the things the prisoner had dropped into his hat, selected a folded piece of paper and spread it upon the desktop where they all saw the stranger's likeness on a wanted poster.

"Murder," read old Forsyth, "robbery, grand theft," the words fell into the silence like steel balls striking glass. Forsyth raised his eyes to Jase. "Beau told me these Hickmans wasn't wanted anywhere."

Jase leaned to look at the flyer. It was very recent, and it had been issued over in Texas, which was a long way from Colorado or Wyoming. "News travels slow," he said, and pointed to a bench. "Sit down, Hickman, and give us some straight answers. Where are your partners?"

The outlaw sat, and said, "What partners?"

Howard Meredith glared. "The ones you bought all those supplies for this evening. That's which partners."

Hickman jumped his eyes from face to face, and ended up looking at the door. Both Mike and Red were standing over there, backs to the door, thumbs hooked in shellbelts, staring at the captive.

"They left," said Hickman. "I give them the grub and they left."

Jase shook his head. "Mister, do you have any idea how much time you have left? This whole damned town's scattering every which way for ropes. That man you shot last night wasn't just some cowboy, it was our

126

local peace officer. He's in the back room right now. You didn't kill him, but that's not going to keep folks from lynching you. You've got a mighty slim chance, but it's the only chance you have. Tell the truth—or when the mob gets here—out the front door you go."

Hickman did not bluster. He lived by the same law. He knew not a man in that room would hesitate to pull on the rope that strangled him. He finally said, "You fellers are going to do it anyway, so the hell with you."

Old Evan Forsyth, the craggy, predictable, entirely guileless wagon maker, shook his head. "Give us all of it, and no one'll take you out of here—without you've had a proper trial. *Don't*—and like Jason said—out the front door you go, like a weasel to a pack of hounds. They'll tear you apart, mister."

Hickman looked longest at Jase. "Ask him what he done with the saddlebags off my brother's saddle. They had the money from a stage robbery up north, plus some pouches of placer gold we took off'n some miners. I figure he's got about five thousand dollars, all told. That's what my brother tried to run off with. Only we caught sight of him and followed."

Jase said, "Which one of you shot him?"

Hickman began wagging his head. "You don't know as much as I figured. We didn't shoot him; we wasn't going to shoot him. All we wanted was that plunder. One of them stage fellers got in a lucky shot." Hickman's cold eyes narrowed. "I know how he died, that old man up at the telegraph office was tellin' it around and I heard it all. And you're Frank Hurd's brother—why don't you tell these men what you done with them saddlebags?"

Jase could feel a slight chill of doubt, of quizzical interest in him, altering the atmosphere. Then Mike

127

Howell spoke up.

"You're crazy," he said in resentful disgust. "*I'm* the one who found your brother first, and he didn't have no saddlebags on his rig. He had a bedroll. He didn't even have a saddle boot." Mike jerked his head sideways. "This here feller, McClure, was the next one to see your brother. Mister Hurd was the last one to the barn. If there'd been any saddlebags, mister, McClure and me'd have found them. There weren't none, and that's the gospel truth."

Evan Forsyth, Clymer and Meredith were standing in silent bafflement, and Jase felt about the same way. Where *were* those saddlebags?

CHAPTER EIGHTEEN

BUT THE ISSUE WAS NOT THE SADDLEBAGS, IT WAS the bushwhacking, and old Evan Forsyth, who was not a man to be sidetracked, hewed to the line when he said, "Why did you shoot Sheriff Beaufort?"

Hickman gave a direct answer, his first one. "I didn't know he was no sheriff. I thought he was Frank Hurd's brother. I'd been watchin' the ranch and seen Hurd a few times. I thought he was riding to town, maybe had the saddlebags with him." Hickman shrugged. "I saw it wasn't Hurd after the feller fell, so I got out of there, and we left a big track, then cut back and raided his ranch." The narrowed, venomous eyes locked on Jase again. "He's good at hiding things, I can tell you that."

"Oh hell," exclaimed Mike Howell. "How many times you got to be told—*there weren't no saddlebags!*"

Jim Forsyth, hat on the back of his head, went back to the earlier question. "Where are your partners, mister?

128

I'm not going to fool around with you. Just once, and you'd better believe me. *Where are they?*"

Hickman started to snarl his answer, but from up the road several men calling back and forth held him suddenly silent. The sound held every man in the room silent, then Jase turned and said, "Mike—Red: Drop that damned bar over the door." The pair of cowboys obeyed at once, then Howard Meredith stepped to a barred front window and craned northward.

He said, "Good Lord! It's the whole town."

Forsyth did not yield to the distraction. "Answer," he snarled at the prisoner. "Where are your partners?"

Hickman was getting pale in the face. He looked frantically from the barred door to the windows, which had steel bars embedded outside the sills. "They're out a mile on the west range, waiting for me to come out there with him." Hickman stabbed at Jase with a finger. "Him." He dropped his hand and swallowed hard. "Keep 'em out of here. Give me a gun, a man's got the right to—"

"Shut up," snapped Jim Forsyth, and turned at the nearer sound of someone in the back room. Without another word Jim went back where Beau had been awakened by the angry voices up the road.

For Jase, the prospect of being besieged inside the jailhouse had very little appeal. He had never faced a mob before, and the sounds outside, coming down the roadway from up in the area of Milner's saloon, were unnerving.

A lot of those men he had never seen before tonight, but there would be just as many, now that word had spread through town that Beau's bushwhacker was at the jailhouse that he *would* know. He had no intention whatsoever of firing his gun at those townsmen. Or even

129

at the others, at the local riders and the Arizonans, out there. Not over someone like Houston Hickman's brother.

When Jim returned from the cell room Jase said, "I'm going after the other two." Young Forsyth frowned.

"What about this one, Jase? They're going to bust in here and lynch him, if they can."

Preacher Clymer, who had said very little up to now, suddenly became a different man. He had inspected the building with a knowledgeable eye, and said, "The whole Secesh army couldn't break in here, unless they had cannon—and there aren't any cannons in Junction." He turned slowly towards Jase. "Take two men—no more, because we'll need the others—and bring back that other pair. Go out the back way and hurry." Clymer smiled. "Don't tarry, my boy don't tarry. The only thing that'll break this up out in the roadway will be a diversion, and you've got to be it. Otherwise, they're going to keep on botherin' us in here. Which two men?"

Jase did not hesitate. "My riders, Howell and McClure."

Clymer was brisk. "Very good. Come along, Mister Forsyth and I'll see you out the back way. You other men—take those rifles and shotguns out of the wall rack and check their loads. Stand ready to repel an assault."

No one questioned Preacher Clymer's orders, and it wasn't young Forsyth, who went quickly with Jase, Red, Mike, and the minister through to the rear doorway, who spoke next, it was Jim Forsyth's father and as he reached to lift the door bar, he said, "Preacher's right, Jase. The only thing that'll keep this from turning into something none of us'll be proud of afterwards, is a diversion. You find them fellers and haul 'em back here, if you got to fetch 'em along by the heels behind your horse."

It was dark in the alleyway and the noise up at the north end of town was growing louder, more like a deep, sullen growl. Jase hesitated only for a moment after the door slammed closed behind him. He heard the oak bar being dropped solidly into place from the inside, and looked at Howell and McClure. They did not even glance at him, they both started southward towards the livery barn at a spirited little trot.

Jase's conscience bothered him until they got down to the barn. It was empty. Not even that cooperative hostler was around. He was probably up with the mob, but Jase did not spend any time worrying about that. He brought forth his horse, rigged it out swiftly, expertly, and vaulted into the saddle. As he rode out into the alleyway with Howell and McClure at his heels, a man appeared from the night and called out.

"Hey, is that you, Homer?"

Jase did not bother replying, he whirled southward and booted his startled horse into a long-legged lope. Behind him his riders did the same, and farther back, in the dark alleyway, that bewildered townsman sang out again: "Hey, what the hell's going on around here tonight?"

Where Jase could do it, finally, he swung west and put the outskirts of town behind him. Then he slackened a little until Mike and Red came up, and as they loped easily along he said, "Maybe Hickman was telling the truth; maybe those other two are out here no more than a mile. I kind of believe he wasn't lying, because if they expected him to fetch me out to them, they wouldn't be too far from town, but where, exactly, is something else again."

"There's a sure way to find out," said Howell. "Split

131

up and sashay back and forth, and if any of us sees a couple of fellers, fire off one round into the air."

McClure muttered: "Into the air, hell; fire off—*at them fellers!*"

Jase agreed, they slowed their horses to a walk, rode a little farther along side by side, then McClure split off first, heading north, and a little farther along Mike Howell also split off. Jase did not deviate, and he had a personal reason for not turning right or left. It had to do with Hickman handing over that sack of supplies to his friends out behind the livery barn, and with the fact that Hickman had left the chestnut gelding down there; his friends, knowing Hickman would be coming towards them from the southerly end of Junction, where he'd left his horse and where they'd been handed up the supplies, would more than likely be due west somewhere.

Hickman hadn't said this might be true, but it did not make sense any other way; men like these outlaws were, did not waste hours riding aimlessly in the night trying to locate one another.

Jase could hear sounds from the town even when he was about a mile away. By twisting in his saddle he could see lights back there, too. More lights than there had been an hour earlier. Junction had been rather thoroughly aroused. What worried him was that, on ahead somewhere, the other pair of outlaws would notice this, too, and might either circle around like wary wolves to see what was happening, or they might decide that whatever it was, they did not like it, and flee.

He straightened forward, probed the night, which had a smoky old lopsided moon to brighten it a little along with a surfeit of stars, and neither saw movement nor heard anything.

His horse's ears were the best telegraph for the kind

of undertaking he was involved in; his horse's ears and nose. He watched the animal for some sign that it might have detected a scent or sound out farther, but the horse simply plodded along, fully awake by now, after having been routed out back at the livery barn, but willing to turn drowsy again, now that it was not being urged to hasten.

Jase had covered more than a mile, perhaps as much as a mile and a half, when he began to have some second thoughts, some serious doubts. He rode back and forth, north and south, and even retraced his route a half mile or so. There was no one anywhere within range of his riding and when he became convinced of that he halted, pushed back his hat, leaned with both hands on top of the saddle horn, and looked slowly all around. Except for the muted tumult back in town, the night was empty. Not just of sound, but of men and horses. He could sense its emptiness.

Finally, he reined northward to seek Mike and Red. Something was definitely wrong.

He found Howell first, and rode right up to pistol range before he saw him standing there, gun barrel resting across his saddle, on the far side of his mount. As soon as Howell managed the recognition he put up the gun, stepped across leather, and said "Well, you can now tell your grandchildren you came within an ace of bein' an angel tonight."

Jase ignored that. "Where's Red?"

Howell jerked a thumb northward. "Up there, I reckon. Why?"

"Did you see or hear anything?"

"Not so much as a coyote," replied Mike. "You?"

"Nothing." Jase reined along northward and Mike fell in beside him. As they rode Jase mentioned a possibility

133

that had occurred to him. "Suppose Hickman was supposed to deliver me—at the ranch."

Mike thought that over, then said, "Why? They'd want you out here somewhere. Goin' all the way back there—"

"If they think I got the saddlebags, and if they couldn't find them when they ransacked the house, Mike, they might think, by delivering me there, I could be made to dig them up. Where would a cowman hide something?"

Mike scratched his nose. "Yeah. He'd bury it where he had a right to bury stuff. All right. Want me to whistle up McClure?"

Jase gave a pained look over that and Howell slouched along saying nothing. When they found Red he had already heard them coming but instead of setting up an ambush the way Mike had done, McClure had begun a wide, circling maneuver. They did not even know he was behind them until, when he recognized their horses from a distance, he called to them.

"What you fellers doin' up here? I thought you said you was going to make a sweep southward."

They waited until Red rode up, then Jase explained his idea, and the three of them turned west and walked their horses along, discussing ways to ascertain if those other two outlaws were actually at the ranch.

Eventually, when they were a goodly distance from town, Jase twisted to glance back. He could make out the lights, still, but the distance was too great to hear sounds. As he hauled back around he said, "I hope those damned fools don't bust in."

McClure and Howell were not too concerned. Mike was biting a chew off his cut plug when he answered that remark. "Let 'em. What difference does it make

134

whether they hang him tonight or next week? He's sure as hell going to hang."

Red agreed. "The trouble with the law is that it don't work right. Justice is for hanging that feller. The law's got to make a big show of a lot of talk and ceremony, then maybe it'll get all bogged down in its own wind and forget all about the hanging."

Jase did not argue with them for a very good reason: he believed they were both right.

They had covered about five miles and had only a short distance to go when Red McClure's black, piercing eyes picked up a flash on ahead, very small and close to the ground. He drew rein at once, then grunted while waiting for the little flash to reappear. It didn't, so he said, "Someone up there about a mile, who is squattin' on the ground, just lit a smoke."

Mike screwed up his face to peer ahead. "You sure?"

McClure answered without taking his eyes off that little black grid of night on ahead. "Well, now, Mike if you'd take to a clean habit like smoking tobacco instead of a dirty one like chawing it, you'd have seen that match flick on, then flick out."

Howell's head snapped around to take exception to this insult but Jase intervened. "Get down. We'll walk ahead and lead the horses until we're a little closer, then we'll off-saddle and leave the horses and finish this on foot. Right now, we don't need the horses to nicker and tell someone up there at the buildings someone is coming."

They dismounted and started onward, concentrating their full attention on the buildings of the Hurd place, which they could not as yet make out in the night.

CHAPTER NINETEEN

SHORT OF GOING INTO THE RANCH YARD THERE WAS NO way to locate those two outlaws. For once the massive buildings, which had been a source of pride to Jase all his life, were being used against him. Out where he and his riders unsaddled and dumped their gear in the grass, it was possible to make out every hulking log silhouette on ahead a short distance, and those men could be anywhere, at the barn, the shoeing shed, the main house, or the bunkhouse.

He might've been encouraged to take a few chances if those had been ordinary range riders, but he had already convinced himself that they were anything but ordinary men, in any sense. One of them was a Hickman. He had no idea who the other one was, except that he had to be another renegade, and men like that were more deadly than rattlesnakes. Neither he nor his two riders were actually in the same class as those men with guns, or at this kind of skulking and maneuvering, but they had one advantage: so far, the outlaws did not know they were just beyond sight of the buildings.

As they released the horses, who ambled away and fell to grazing, McClure sidled up and said, "We didn't do this right, Boss. We should have brought a posse out from town.

Jase did not reply; if McClure had thought that over he'd have appreciated that there was no way actually, to entice anyone out of town. What those men from Milner's saloon wanted was to hang Beau's bushwhacker, and even had it been possible to make them believe there were two more outlaws involved, they still wouldn't have left town until they'd done the

136

other little job first.

Mike Howell, standing there chewing thoughtfully, finally made a suggestion. "One of us has got to sneak down closer. Not much point in standing out here all night waitin' for someone to light up another smoke."

Jase agreed, but he began having doubts about himself as a strategist. He had never before been involved in anything like this. His father had, back in the early days when Indians raided the range. And Frank, too, probably would have known how to handle it, but even if Frank could have been there, he probably would have been on the other side.

McClure said, "If all three of us could get down in back of the shoeing shed, maybe we could sing out and make 'em give up."

Mike groaned. "Red, in the first place, them fellers is gunmen, and wanted ones at that. They'd shoot their way clear. In the second place, they got their horses with 'em and even if they got scairt, they wouldn't give up, they'd head out the back way, westward. In the third place—"

"Wait a minute," murmured Jase. "The horses." His riders looked around at him. "Get some stones and slip round our horses and get them to running towards the yard. That ought to stir them up, hearing horses coming on the run."

At once Mike and Red bent over and scuffed for stones. Jase did, too, then the three of them hiked out and around their freed animals, got them aligned for the charge, and pelted them with stones. It worked, but probably as much because the horses wanted to run towards the corrals out back of the barn, which they associated with feed, as much as because the JH men got them aimed in that direction.

Jase then led his riders in an ungainly lope on foot down towards the yard, keeping the shoeing shed and that old canvas topped wagon between themselves and the onward yard.

It worked very well. By the time they flattened behind the shoeing shed someone over at the barn called in a subdued, harsh voice to someone else, "Can you see 'em, Cal? Take cover!"

The running animals made a big half-circle around the barn towards the corrals. Jase could hear them snort when they slid to a stiff-legged halt back there. The snort probably meant that the horses had smelled strangers in the barn's vicinity.

Jase slipped away from the shed to the far side of the wagon, dropped low and peered in the direction of the barn from under the wagon's running gear. McClure and Howell came up soundlessly and dropped to all fours to do the same.

There was no sight of movement over there, so evidently "Cal" and his partner had indeed taken cover. Jase said they would be towards the back of the barn, probably, trying to make out the loose stock. Mike was sardonic about that.

"Maybe. But there ain't no way to be sure without crossing the yard—and that'd be like committing suicide."

Jase drew back, got upright and leaned upon the tailgate of the wagon, studying the barn area. There *was* a way, but it was admittedly risky, and it would take some time. The time element, he did not believe, was going to matter. Those men were accustomed to waiting, and were in fact doing it now; as for the risk— unless they gave up, which they'd have no intention of doing—there would be risk even if they just sat down

138

and waited for daybreak.

He said, "Mike, slip off to the right; go out as far as you've got to, to keep them from being able to see or hear you, then come back southward where you can see both the front and back of the barn. You understand that?"

Howell nodded.

"Red, you do the same, only you go to the left, up around the main house and back down until you're between the barn and the bunkhouse. Watch the front and back. If they fort up in there, we can out wait them. If they try and make a break for it out the front or back, we can nail them."

McClure understood. "Where you goin' to be? The bad part about somethin' like this is that one of us might mistake one of the others for them fellers. It's happened before."

"I'm going to stay right here where I can see down through the barn. I'll allow a half hour for you fellers to get set, then I'm going to holler for them to come out, just once, and open up; see if I can't ground sluice them down the alleyway of the barn."

Howell wasn't too hopeful. "What you'd need for that would be a shotgun or a rifle, and we ain't got neither."

"What I need," corrected Jase, "is about ten more men—*with* rifles and scatterguns. But we don't have 'em. Head out, both of you, and be damned careful. Those aren't cowboys in there; they can out shoot any of us. You'd better remember that."

Howell left first, slipping away in a rearward crouch until he was out of sight, then McClure, with better cover to the left, also slipped away. Jase, left quite alone, checked his Colt, replaced it loosely in the holster and leaned on the wagon staring into the dark big old barn. By now, the outlaws had discovered that those were loose horses. There was a chance they might have got close enough to also make out that they were horses that had recently been ridden, but that was not too strong a possibility; range horses, regardless of how well broke they were, did not permit strangers to get very close to them when they were free, especially in the night.

Jase actually had no strategy, and even if he did nothing until daybreak he could still rely upon surprise. But there had been that admonition back at the jailhouse to add pressure: they needed a diversion in town to take away the danger to the men locked inside.

The longer he stood there the more he wished it would be possible to wait until the outlaws in the barn made the first move. Eventually, they were bound to get impatient.

But that was not possible, not as long as that trouble back in town more or less depended upon his intervention. He studied the sky and was surprised to find the moon down as far as it was. He did not carry a watch or he'd have verified the lateness. For some reason, he'd felt all along it was still early. It wasn't, not according to that descending moon.

The half hour expired. He waited a little longer to be absolutely certain his riders would be in position, then he stepped to the tailgate of the wagon again and was ready to sacrifice their advantage by calling out. He even drew his sixgun to follow up his yell with bullets.

Abruptly a man appeared on horseback over across the yard in the doorless big barn opening. Behind him Jase could dimly make out another man, at least he could make out movement as though a second rider were stepping up, as though he whirled his horse as he hit the seating leather.

Jase was too startled to react immediately. Caution made him wonder if perhaps those two hadn't discovered that they were being flanked, and had decided to make a run for it. By the time it occurred to him that the outlaws had probably become impatient and had decided to head back towards town to see what might be keeping their partner, that second horseman rode forward. Jase saw that one lean to speak. They were both momentarily motionless, surveying the roundabout yard and night.

Jase sang out. "Hold it right where you are!"

He might as well have yelled for them to run for it. They reacted like a pair of lobo wolves; without even seeming to look over where that call had come from both men hooked their horses, hard, and as the astonished animals sprang ahead, both outlaws went for their guns.

Jase had an edge since his gun was already in his hand, but even so, as he threw up and fired the foremost outlaw also fired, and he'd had to draw. What Jase had thought earlier, about neither he nor his riders being equal to men like these in this kind of a situation, was proved then and there. But the outlaw only fired in Jase's general direction because he had not seen his enemy, and when Jase fired from a distance of about a hundred feet, he did not miss. The outlaw threw up both arms, dropped his pistol, then sagged ahead and tried to grab the horn, missed, tried for the mane and missed that too, and disappeared down the off-side of his horse, where the second outlaw's mount had to react in a split second and jump over the body as it struck the yard.

The second man fired twice, and both shots made splinters fly from the wagon's tailgate. Very good gunmanship considering that the outlaw was on top of the hurricane deck of a panicking horse whose each forward jump was high, longer, and hit down harder.

Jase flinched back both times, then sprang round front of the wagon in a reckless moment to get in his next shot. From over on the north side of the bunkhouse Red McClure let go a blast that was followed a second later by another blast. Jase was tracking the rider's night-gloomed silhouette when McClure did that again, fired once, then again, almost before the reverberations from his first shot had ceased. That time the second man went off his horse's back.

Ten seconds later the only sound was a very distant cadence made by two free-running saddled horses. The last echo had departed.

Jase leaned on the tailgate and reloaded before stepping out into the yard. Evidently McClure did the same thing, because eventually, when Mike Howell came walking up through the barn from out back and halted in the front opening to survey the two lumpy silhouettes strung out between the barn and the main house, he was the first one to show himself and to speak. Mike was disgusted. He walked over to the pair of outlaws with his cocked Colt in hand and looked at them.

"Why'n hell didn't you fellers let me know they was goin' to charge out'n there?" he demanded of Red and Jase, as soon as the latter men walked into sight.

Jase's reply was forthright. "I didn't even know for a fact they were in there, until I moved up to holler towards the barn—and there they were, mounted and heading out."

Mike put up his gun, leaned and rolled the man Jase had shot over on to his back. Still disgusted, Mike said,

"Dead as a lousy mackerel." He went to the other one, but McClure was already down on one knee over there. Red looked at Jase and said, "This one ain't."

McClure was right. The second man, who looked about forty years old in the poor light, lean and wolfish, and who resembled Houston Hickman very noticeably, had been knocked from his horse by a bullet that had broken his right leg up high, and by a second bullet that had pierced his chest up under the collarbone. He was lying there making gasping sounds.

Jase turned to Mike. "Rig up the buckboard and throw some straw in back. Red, get some rags so's we can stop the bleeding. Then we've got to get this pair back to town."

As his men scattered Jase knelt beside the gasping man. "You'll be all right," he said, "if you don't leak out too much blood."

The outlaw looked up, his face twisted with pain. "My leg's busted," he gasped.

Jase regarded the man, saw the shock, and also saw that the outlaw did not even know he had been shot in the body. "We'll tie off the leg, mister, just lie back and take it easy."

The outlaw strained to find his partner and Jase pushed him back down. "I said lie easy. Your partner's dead. What was his name?"

"Cal Coulter."

Jase nodded. "Then you're Hickman."

The outlaw nodded. "Yeh. Who're you—the law?"

They looked at one another, then Hickman sank flat and lost consciousness.

CHAPTER TWENTY

THEY GOT HICKMAN'S BROKEN LEG TIED OFF TO STOP the bleeding and boosted him into the wagon on top of the straw. His body puncture did not seem to be bleeding much, at least, not outwardly. There was nothing, really, that they could do about that. Jase said perhaps Preacher Clymer could help Hickman.

The dead man they dumped in, too, without much ceremony, then Jase stirred up the team and headed for town at a trot. He'd have gone faster if he hadn't been worried about Hickman.

Still, they made it in less than an hour, which was fairly good time considering that they had to cover almost six miles.

Junction was as quiet as a tomb when they drove in at the upper end. There was still lights on, though, in some of the stores and residences, and Milner's saloon was as bright as before. It also seemed as full of men, inside and outside, in little groups, standing around. The jailhouse was dark, and that gave Jase a bad feeling as he tooled the wagon down the center of the road past the saloon, where at least fifteen armed men turned, without speaking or moving, to stare.

There were three men standing out front of the darkened jailhouse. One was that sly drinker who worked down at the livery barn, but he was stone sober now. The other two were cowboys, both calmly smoking cigarettes as Jase pulled up at the tie rack and climbed down, along with Mike and Red McClure. One of the cowboys ambled over, looked into the wagon, gasped, then called and the other two men came over to also look in, to stare.

Jase used his pistol barrel to rap on the jailhouse door and to call out his name. Preacher Clymer opened the door, smiling. He had a sawed-off shotgun in his hands.

Jase stepped in and peered around. The room did not look bullet-pocked and over at the stove Meredith and the elder Forsyth were having a cup of black coffee in the gloom. Forsyth regarded Jase calmly. "You get 'em, boy?" he demanded.

Jase nodded, jerking a thumb towards the door. "One's dead, one's shot up pretty bad." He turned. "Preacher . . . ?" Clymer handed Jase the shotgun and without a word went outside. McClure, who had entered with Jase, turned and barred the door.

Jim Forsyth, who was at a window, said, "Quiet night, Jase." He looked over. "Maybe we can light the lamp now."

His father moved to do that as Jim, leaning upon a rifle, said, "We cut loose with four shotgun blasts and they went back up to George's saloon like Old Nick was breathing down the back of their necks. That was an hour ago. They been standing around up there, trying to take on a load of Dutch courage ever since."

Clymer banged on the door, Red opened it, and Preacher, with those idlers from outside, barged in carrying the wounded outlaw. They took him wordlessly on through into the back room to a bunk in a cell adjoining Beau's cell. Howard Meredith looked anxious. "How bad is he?" he asked no one in particular, and Jase told them what had happened at the ranch. Meredith put down his coffee cup and went along to look at the injured man. So did old Forsyth, and as soon as those two were gone, Jim said, "Jase, the evening coach come in a little while ago. Tassie was on

145

it—with a little boy. We could see George Milner taking them over towards the Meredith place. Maybe you'd want to go over there."

Jase did, indeed, want to go over there, but not quite yet. "Where's the bushwhacker, Jim?" he asked, because there was no sign of Hickman in the office.

"Locked up in the back room. He got kind of noisy when the ruckus started, so I pitched him in and locked him up. Didn't like the idea of having one of them behind me all the time. Much of a fight at the ranch, Jase?"

Now that it all seemed about to end, Jase thought back. "Not really," he replied. "It happened so damned fast. I don't figure it was over twenty seconds from start to finish."

Forsyth smiled. "Yeah, that's about how it was here. A lot of boys out there waving ropes and shooting in the air, and when we let fly, they took off like a covey of quail."

Meredith and the elder Forsyth returned, picked up their coffee cups and looked gravely over at Jase. Then Meredith cleared his throat. "Jason, who is that little boy my daughter brought back with her?"

Jase winced inside. They were all looking at him. He would much preferred to have kept that to himself, but as he thought about it, it became increasingly clear that keeping this kind of a secret after all that had happened since his brother had been brought back to be buried, was impossible.

"My nephew." he said, and looked each one of them in the eye waiting for the next question. No one asked it. No one had to.

Clymer appeared. "Beau wants to see you, Jason."

There were two lights in the jailhouse now, one in the

146

office, another one in the back room where Clymer was working over his latest patient. When Jase walked into Beau's cell the sheriff smiled through a dark stubble of beard. "Been a busy night," he said, sounding stronger than he'd sounded at their last meeting.

Jase drew up the little stool and related all that had happened between the time he left the jailhouse and the time he returned. Beau was interested in every word, but when Jase finished Beau did not mention the fighting, he said, "I heard 'em talking about Tassie getting home, Jase. I got the rest of it from Hickman across the hall in that cell yonder. I mean about the little boy, Frank's kid . . . You figuring on taking him out to the ranch with you?"

Jase nodded. "I didn't know she'd bring him back, though."

"No reason for her not to," said Beau. "His mother died couple months ago and Hickman said they gave him to some neighbors."

Jase was shocked. "She died? But I thought . . ." He rose, walked out of the cell, crossed the little corridor and looked in where Beau's ambusher was sitting hunched on a wall bunk smoking. Hickman looked up, venomously.

"Did you shoot my brother?" he snarled, and Jase didn't bother to answer that.

"When did your sister die, Hickman?"

The outlaw shrugged. "Month, six weeks ago, what difference does it make?"

"What did she die of ?"

"Tuberculosis. What's it to you?"

"I'm going to raise Frank's kid, that's what it is to me."

Hickman turned away. "I don't give a damn what you do with Frank's kid," he snarled, and kept his back to

147

Jase.

Beau had heard all this, and as Jase turned he said, "Why don't you go on over to the Meredith place, Jase? There's no need for you to hang around here any more . . . But there's one thing: what do you reckon come of those saddlebags off the other Hickman's saddle; the ones with that four or five thousand dollars in them?"

Jase looked around. At that moment someone's saddlebags, even if they were stuffed with wealth, meant less than nothing to him. "Don't worry about it, Beau, when Mike and Red have caught up on their sleep, we'll backtrack and find them. Houston hid them sure as hell; maybe he figured he wasn't going to make it, or maybe he figured his brothers and Coulter were going to overtake him. The only thing I'm positive of is that he didn't have them when he got to my barn. We'll go saddlebag hunting in a few days. Right now—well—I'll look in on you maybe tomorrow."

Out front, some of the men from up at Milner's saloon had drifted down where the two Forsyths and Howard Meredith were talking to them in the doorway. As Jase shouldered through without speaking and reached the sidewalk, the men parted to let him pass through. Old Archer Grant was there and as Jase stepped past, Archer said, "Say, Jason, you did right well tonight, but I'm right interested in some saddlebags chock full of money that Hickman feller was supposed to have had. What could you tell us about them?"

Jase halted in mid-stride, turned, looked sulphurously at the telegrapher for a moment, then reached, hoisted old Archer two feet off the ground, turned and marched up where the public water trough stood on the west side of the road, and threw Archer in.

At first, the onlookers were too stunned to speak.

148

Then Red McClure burst out laughing, and that triggered it; everyone, even old Evan Forsyth and Howard Meredith, bent over laughing.

Jase did not look back. He crossed the road and hiked to the farthest corner, swung right and went down to the Meredith house. Tassie was waiting for him. How she knew he'd be along was a mystery, but she was in the parlor and when he knuckled the door she opened it, smiled, and stepped back.

The little boy was fast asleep on a big leather sofa. He hardly stirred when Jason, with Tassie leading him over by the hand, crossed the room and looked down.

She said, "His mother died, Jason. The people his uncles gave him to were delighted at a chance to get rid of him. They told me they had only taken him because they were afraid of the Hickmans, were afraid not to take him."

Jase studied the child. He was very fair, with taffy hair and a suntanned complexion. Frank had been darker, with dark hair and eyes. Tassie pushed a small tintype into Jase's hand. It showed a fair woman, no more than a girl, actually, looking out at him with level blue eyes, a pretty, soft face, and an expression of something like bewilderment. He said, "Elsie?"

Tassie gave the correct name. "Elsa. Elsa Hickman the year she met Frank—and went away with him. She was seventeen."

Jase handed back the picture and looked around. He didn't know exactly what to say. "I'm right obliged to you, Tassie, for fetching him—home."

She smiled. "That's what I went up there for, isn't it? That's what you wanted, Jase." She squeezed his hand. "I told him all about you, about the ranch, even about Junction, on the ride back. He thinks you're wonderful

149

already and he hasn't even seen you."

Now, Jase knew what to say. "Not me, Tass, you." She looked into his eyes, then started to withdraw her hand. He closed his fingers around her palm and held her. "I'm going to need some help."

She looked at the sleeping child. "Yes, you are. You're going to need a *lot* of help."

". . . You?"

She raised her face to him, slowly. "Me, of course, Jason." She squeezed again, and this time he squeezed back. Then she freed her fingers and went over to stand near the big front window beside the doorway. "Do you care what people say?" she asked, her back to him.

He didn't quite understand. "About what? You mean, about me being Frank's brother?"

"No. About me coming out to the ranch every day or so. That's the kind of thing people talk about, isn't it?"

He looked from the sleeping child to her back. "Not where I can hear it, they hadn't better. And not about the lad either—about him being Frank Hurd's boy."

She turned. "He won't be Frank Hurd's boy, Jason. He'll be your boy and my boy. That's how he's going to grow up."

Jase regarded her with the let-down, the delayed reaction from all he'd been through over the past twenty-four hours, finally beginning to catch up with him. He felt tired and strained and old, and even despite all this, she still looked to him like the most beautiful woman he had even seen. Not a girl, a woman. If she'd ever been a girl it had to have been before she met his brother, because even after *that* happened, she hadn't been able to be a girl, she'd been forced into becoming a woman. Strain and heartache made girls turn into women overnight.

"Tassie—you reckon, maybe, that one of these days, somehow or other, possibly . . ."

Her father walked in with his shellbelt and gun slung over one shoulder. He looked at them, looked at the sleeping child, then said, "Honey, if you're up to it, I'd sure take kindly to a hot cup of black coffee maybe laced with a dram or two of that Irish whiskey under the sink in the kitchen. Jason wouldn't turn that down either, I don't believe."

Tassie stood gazing at Jase throughout all this, then she smiled softly at him as she left the room to obey her father, and Jase had his answer to the question he had never quite got around to forming and saying.

Howard Meredith gazed a long while at the child. "They told me at the jailhouse," he ultimately said, and went to drop his bulk into a large chair. "Sit down, Jase. I'm dog-tired and I didn't do much tonight, so you must be twice that tired . . . ? Well, what'll you do, take the child to the ranch?"

Jase sat. "Yes. We're kin, Mister Meredith, and he doesn't have any other."

The older man sighed. "*Neither* of you have any other, Jase." Meredith's hooded, grey gaze fastened upon Jason. "What about Tassie? I mean, were you maybe figuring on . . . talking to her? I know she went to Cheyenne because of you. I know you two've met a few times lately."

"Yes, sir, I—am figuring on talking to her."

Meredith nodded. "You have my blessing, Jase . . . Only I was figuring she might . . . it doesn't matter, really. When I get tired of it, I'll just sell the damned store."

When Tassie returned with their coffee both men looked at her, and both noticed the slight, radiant blush

151

she showed when she smiled and set their tray and cups down.

We hope that you enjoyed reading this
Sagebrush Large Print Western.
If you would like to read more Sagebrush titles,
ask your librarian or contact the Publishers:

United States and Canada

Thomas T. Beeler, *Publisher*
Post Office Box 659
Hampton Falls, New Hampshire 03844-0659
(800) 818-7574

United Kingdom, Eire, and
the Republic of South Africa

Isis Publishing Ltd
7 Centremead
Osney Mead
Oxford OX2 0ES England
(01865) 250333

Australia and New Zealand

Bolinda Publishing Pty. Ltd.
17 Mohr Street
Tullamarine, 3043, Victoria, Australia
(016103) 9338 0666